MADDER MUSIC

Peter De Vries was born in Chicago of Dutch immigrant parents and was educated in Dutch Reformed Calvinist schools. He graduated from Calvin College in 1931 and held the post of editor, for a short time, of a community newspaper in Chicago. He then supported himself with a number of different jobs, including those of vending-machine operator, toffee-apple salesman, radio actor, furniture mover, lecturer to women's clubs, and associate editor of *Poetry*. In 1943 he managed to lure James Thurber to Chicago to give a benefit lecture for *Poetry*, and Thurber suggested that De Vries should write for *The New Yorker*. He did. Before long he was given a part-time editorial position on that magazine, dropped his other activities, and moved to New York City. He has remained on the editorial staff of *The New Yorker* ever since. Peter De Vries is the author of some twenty novels, the most recent being *Sauce for the Goose*. Penguin Books also publishes his *Consenting Adults, or The Duchess Will Be Furious; Forever Panting;* and *The Tunnel of Love*. Peter De Vries lives in Westport, Connecticut, with his wife, Katinka Loeser.

BOOKS BY PETER DE VRIES

NO BUT I SAW THE MOVIE

THE TUNNEL OF LOVE

COMFORT ME WITH APPLES

THE MACKEREL PLAZA

THE TENTS OF WICKEDNESS

THROUGH THE FIELDS OF CLOVER

THE BLOOD OF THE LAMB

REUBEN, REUBEN

LET ME COUNT THE WAYS

THE VALE OF LAUGHTER

THE CAT'S PAJAMAS & WITCH'S MILK

MRS. WALLOP

INTO YOUR TENT I'LL CREEP

WITHOUT A STITCH IN TIME

FOREVER PANTING

THE GLORY OF THE HUMMINGBIRD

I HEAR AMERICA SWINGING

MADDER MUSIC

CONSENTING ADULTS, OR THE DUCHESS WILL BE FURIOUS

SAUCE FOR THE GOOSE

Madder Music

Peter De Vries

PENGUIN BOOKS

Penguin Books Ltd, Harmondsworth,
Middlesex, England
Penguin Books, 625 Madison Avenue,
New York, New York 10022, U.S.A.
Penguin Books Australia Ltd, Ringwood,
Victoria, Australia
Penguin Books Canada Limited, 2801 John Street,
Markham, Ontario, Canada L3R 1B4
Penguin Books (N.Z.) Ltd, 182–190 Wairau Road,
Auckland 10, New Zealand

First published in the United States of America by
Little, Brown and Company, Inc., 1977
First published in Canada by
Little, Brown & Company (Canada) Limited 1977
First published in Great Britain by Victor Gollancz Ltd 1978
Published in Penguin Books in the United States of America by
arrangement with Little, Brown and Company, Inc.
Published in Penguin Books 1982

LIBRARY OF CONGRESS CATALOGING IN PUBLICATION DATA
De Vries, Peter.
Madder music.
I. Title.
PS3507.E8673M3   1982   813'.52   81-19994
ISBN 0 14 00.6133 9   AACR2

Printed in the United States of America by
Offset Paperback Mfrs., Inc., Dallas, Pennsylvania
Set in Linotype Caledonia

The author is grateful for permission to reprint lines from "Dirge Without
Music" from *Collected Poems* by Edna St. Vincent Millay. Copyright 1929
by Edna St. Vincent Millay. Copyright © Norma Millay Ellis, 1956.
Published by Harper & Row, Publishers, Inc.

I cried for madder music and for stronger wine.

— ERNEST DOWSON
"Non Sum Qualis Eram Bonae
Sub Regno Cynarae"

The Fugue

One

"A FUGUE," Dr. Josko explained to her, "is a pathological amnesiac condition during which the patient is apparently conscious of his actions but on return to normal life has no recollection of them. There's more to your husband's case than that, however. In addition to forgetting who he is, he's become somebody else altogether, adopted an entirely new identity for himself. Like that crab, what is it, the hermit crab, that inhabits the shell of another creature, some univalve he finds handy." Dr. Josko was already seeing this as a paper to be delivered at an early psychiatric convention. "And his conviction that he is this other person grows stronger by the day. That makes his behavior doubly deserving of the name fugue, which comes, as you know, from the Latin word for flight. Your husband is fleeing some reality or other, internal or external. He's running away from something out there" — the doctor extended an arm to indicate the world in general — "or in here."

Mrs. Swirling was sure he had laid his hand on his breast only after checking in time the impulse to tap his skull, thus sparing her uneasy subliminal associations with such concepts as "belfry," "upper story," and "fruitcake." The delicacy left them free to regard her husband as a troubled spirit rather than a man gone round the bend.

"You think then that he's a case of split personality?"

"Well, in cases of dual identity the patient may shuttle back and forth between the one and the other. Such cases are rare, but far from nonexistent. That would be no piece of cake to live with. But a man taking total refuge in an adopted, or fictitious, persona is even harder to tunnel into. If your husband would pop back into his normal self, even just for a bit, it would give us a chance to dig into what's bugging him. The split personalities are of course connected at some deeper level. Think of two seemingly separate icebergs which nevertheless underwater are one. It's hard to conduct interviews with the half of him that's" — the word could no longer be shied away from — "delusion."

"You're convinced then that there's no doubt about the diagnosis," Becky Swirling said. "I mean it's not a question of feigning, or anything like that."

"No. It's become quite clear to all of us here at Silver Slopes who've talked to him. None of us has any doubt that we are dealing with a bona fide case of mental delusion. Your husband thinks he's Groucho Marx."

"With all that that implies."

"With all that that implies."

As if to remind them both precisely what they meant by that, he rose and beckoned her to an open window, through which had floated, from time to time in the course of their conversation, fragmentary but solid confirmations of the problem. A figure in a black tailcoat, wearing greasepaint mustache and eyebrows and wire spectacles, and flourishing a big cigar, bustled about the grounds in a bent-over position,

4

darting for the most part from woman to woman, striking up conversations often as not abandoned as soon as begun, though occasionally pausing to drop a flirtatious remark or make some amorous overture, usually accompanied by a grin and a suggestive jiggling of the eyebrows. As they watched, he pursued a nurse, overtaking her on the walk just below their window.

"How about dinner sometime?" he chattered in a remarkable simulation of his model's voice and cadence, giving the cigar a flick. "Will you be my girl Friday? I'm booked up Saturday and Sunday and most of the next week. Perhaps I might tuck you in the following weekend, and I do mean tuck you in, if I may end a sentence with a proposition . . ." The nurse disappeared through the front door, but he readily found a patient to accost, a large blond woman in a red cape. "You must be crazy to stay here. At these prices. And they're going up. I have inside information, so if you'll just step inside — preferably to my room . . ." The woman's stroll took them momentarily out of sight behind a clump of rhododendrons, from which they presently emerged into view again, she quickening her pace and he pattering in her wake with coattails flying. "— you'll find me broad-minded, in fact it's all I think about." Some more than verbal liberty may have been taken behind the screen of foliage, because the woman stopped, turned, and said with some spirit, "Just who do you think you are?"

"She must never go to the movies," Dr. Josko murmured. "But it's absolutely uncanny. The impersonation. Not just the voice but that exact New York pronunciation. And the facial expressions. To say nothing of that crouch. And the fact that the mustache and eyebrows are greasepaint only heightens the illusion, because that's what Groucho himself wore."

"And as a Groucho buff he could probably tell you the exact date he started it. Late for a show or something and instead of wasting time putting on the eyebrows and mustache he just snatched up a grease stick and presto — it became permanent," Becky Swirling said.

The doctor shook his head in wonderment. "Well, it beats Napoleons and Hitlers and messianic complexes."

"You have your share of those?"

"No, not really. But we did have a man here once who thought he was Washington Irving. A modest enough little megalomania."

A tall man in a dark suit came down the stairs and accosted the patient with a document of some sort.

"Olmstead, our cashier. I've instructed him to buttonhole him with the bill he's running up any chance he gets. Just to see if there's any sense of reality whatever. Let's see what happens."

The scene was again close enough to the window for them to hear as well as watch. Groucho bent to scrutinize the statement a moment, then tossed his head in a devil-may-care manner.

"Oh, let's not trouble ourselves with anything so sordid as money, shall we? You know my motto. Never put off till tomorrow what you can postpone indefinitely." He began to dance and sing, whirling his legs about in circles. "Since I've been to my broker I've never been broker. I owe everybody, I owe. I owe everybooooody, I owe! Well, I must be off. *You* must be off, thinking I'd pay these rates. And they call it free association. Huh! But I shan't keep you, you must have a thousand things to do. I'll bet the ladies just adore that great big Kirk Douglas dimple in your chin. I thought at first it might be your navel, everything is so high these days."

The subject darted obliquely off across the grass, hightailing it toward a tall, burly woman in a green pants suit. Trailing her in what had become a habitual jackknifed posture he said, "My friend wanted to bet me ten dollars I

6

couldn't pick you up, and he's probably right. You must weigh two hundred and fifty pounds if you're a day. Do you mind if I run around you a couple of times? That'll be like jogging once around the grounds." The incessant hyperkinetic predatory bustle next had him veering toward a lanky man in a cowboy shirt with a string tie, who was chewing a wad of tobacco. "I caught your act in that psychodrama session the other night. Has anybody ever told you you ought to be on the stage? There's one leaving in an hour, and you'd better be on it, podner." Affecting a bowlegged gait by walking on the sides of his feet he shambled toward a black youth strumming a banjo on a nearby bench. "How many times have Ah told you to quit pickin' that banjo and git out thah and pick that cotton." He skipped away, swinging his arms as he sang. "Con — stantinople. M-i-s-s-i-s-s-i-p-p-i."

"A seemingly deep-seated need to outrage," Dr. Josko mused, twisting the venetian-blind cord in his fingers as they watched from the window. "Telling off the cockeyed world, uncorking God knows what bottled up inside. Tell me, has he ever behaved like that in real life? Scandalizing people? Vindictive in any sense?"

Mrs. Swirling answered with solemn simplicity:

"He was a pussycat. He was the friendliest, gentlest man I know. Around the house the soul of consideration. Couldn't do enough for you. But, um."

"Yes? But what?"

"He did stray. Not that I'm in any position to — I mean I was the Other Woman in his first marriage, as well as the wronged wife in ours. Without a perfect record of my own there either. You know it's all musical beds these days. As a friend of the family I used to see how nice he was around the house with the first Mrs. Swirling. Just a pussycat, pitching in with the dirty work. Like he didn't see why anybody who cooked a meal should clean up after it too. Looking back

7

now, maybe it was guilt about his affairs that made him so doubly peachy at home."

Dr. Josko enjoyed few things more than coining an epigram. But he positively shimmered with pleasure when he felt a paradox coming on.

"Yes. Nothing will make a man a model husband faster than infidelity."

He took his pretty visitor intently in to see whether he had scored. She was looking out again at the figure scurrying among the lilac bushes, from whose white and purple blossoms a fresh May wind gently winnowed the scent.

"So he probably kept all that hostility repressed," the doctor said. "The lid's been blown off it now all right. He has, in fine, flipped."

"At least you can't say 'suffering from delusions.' *He's* feeling no pain."

"That's precisely the purpose of many a psychosis, at least of this variety. To feel no pain. The patient achieves biochemical peace at the price of his reason. A drastic degree of the decerebration we all engage in to some extent to — well, the more to enjoy life or the better to endure it, depending on which end of Dr. Johnson's famous stick you figure you've got a hold of. You might even call it a way of pulling himself together." The doctor sighed heavily. "And the purpose of therapy is to reverse the transaction. Get the patient to purchase back his reason at the price of his tranquillity. Some job! There are times when I wouldn't want to be in my shoes. This is going to be a tough nut to crack. Oh, I'm so sorry."

"That's all right. But, um, speaking of shoes, how would you like to be in mine, with all those bills running up? I simply haven't the — My husband has some, well, I think one thing of value. A painting. Do you know Jawlensky?"

"I'm . . . not . . ."

8

"I'd need time to sell it of course. I obviously can't take him home with me now, though I know he's making a shambles of the sanatarium."

"Let's let the meter click for a while. I'm interested enough in the case. Fascinated I might say." The doctor turned back into the room, rolling his lower lip between thumb and forefinger as he often did when deep in thought. "Now, you haven't seen him today yet. Let's do the visit the other way around this time. Have him come in here, and see how he behaves, what gives. Sit down a moment yet. I want to kick a few things around with you first. You say your husband has had this lifelong obsession with Groucho Marx. A thing about him, as they say today."

"So I gather, though, um, I'm not the best authority on my husband. I've only been married to him a little over a year, and supposed to be getting a divorce. But yes, he has a collection of — how would you say it? Grouchoiana? That's probably second only to the stuff of Groucho's that's gone to the Library of Congress. Bob asked to see the collection when he was in Washington once. And so forth and so on."

She watched the portly doctor walk the office, erectly and solemnly, as though he were on sentinel duty.

"His choice of alter ego couldn't have been more perfect, or for his purposes, more cunning. The most famous comic of our time is a walking, or I should say prowling, testimonial for Sigmund Freud. What does Freud find the two basic human drives most released in humor? Sex and aggression. And what is Groucho's chief stock-in-trade? Lechery and insult. My guess is that under hypnosis, which I'm going to start today, incidentally, we'll find those two drives very strong in his own makeup. So strong that he needs a surrogate to express them more freely than he could himself within the bounds of anything we could remotely call polite society. Hostility and desire. He wants to hit every man he

9

knows and possess every woman he sees. Let's just perform a little experiment now, or test. I'll — You say he's yet given no sign of recognizing you."

"None whatever. But that's what I meant a while ago by feigning —"

"No, no, let's forget that aspect of it. There's a level at which everything like this is feigning, just as all catatonic stupor is in part pseudo-stupor. Never mind that now. I'll ask him in here, and in less time than it takes to tell it he'll be insulting me and making a play for you. That's been the pattern and I'll stake my professional reputation he'll follow it here. But one thing: you never know when somebody will snap out of a fugue. I'm sure he's not ready to recognize you yet. Instead he'll ogle and sidle and sniff around you — a la Groucho." Circling the desk, the doctor now slowly summed up the case as he saw it, as though talking to himself. "The patient has deep-seated resentments against people, against life itself, along with probably guilt-ridden sexual impulses (I've learned he had a strong religious upbringing). Together they make a combination he can't give adequate expression to as Robert Swirling, but can unload with impunity as Groucho Marx. Anything he wants to get away with he can pin on Groucho. All right. When he gets here, play along with him. I gather you've helped him at home with his, er, routines."

"As long as I've known him he's been promising to do his imitation at charity balls and things, but nothing ever came of it. Until this NAACP benefit where he cracked up. I wasn't there, I was . . ." Becky Swirling smiled in a way the doctor noted as characteristic of her, with her closed mouth twisted to one side. It gave her momentarily the look of a mischievous child. "I was having a sort of nervous tailspin myself. I guess we're rather a hairy pair."

"I see. But how amazing his was, how neat. He goes on from the impersonation into the actual delusion. What a bridge! What a way to leave the real world! Hide in the role you're playing, stay there, curl up in it. But go on. You helped him polish up his material."

She nodded. "For a while we even toyed with the idea of my doing it with him — stooging for him. I used to be — well, I guess I'm what you'd call an actress *manquée*." The doctor inclined his head with a vaguely sympathetic expression, again noting the wryly charming smile. "I do a pretty good Bette Davis myself. But I'm no Margaret Dumont — thank God!"

The doctor looked blank.

"That dowager type Groucho played off of in all those movies. He says to this day she never understood any of the lines. Including that famous one in *Duck Soup*, remember, where Groucho says to his brothers, 'Remember you're fighting for her honor, which is more than she ever did.' He claims she never understood that."

The doctor laughed. "Well, it's no matter you're no Margaret Dumont — I remember her now of course. The thing is, play along with him when he gets here." He was becoming visibly excited by the impending encounter. "Feed him lines you tried out with him at home, all you can recall, or work in. Because — and I can't emphasize this strongly enough — *it may forge our first link with his real self by making him recognize you at last*. That would be a real breakthrough. Take us on our first step toward finding out what it is he's trying to forget."

This time she lowered her head and smiled into her hands.

"Maybe it's me. He's trying to forget. Things got pretty kinky between us." He waited for her to go on. She only looked up and concluded, "But I'm game. Go ahead. Send for him if you think it — think there's any percentage in it."

Just as the doctor let Groucho in the door the telephone rang, and Groucho bustled straight on across the office toward it. "I'll get it, Doc," he said, plucking it from its cradle. He tilted back in the swivel chair with his feet on the desk. "Hello . . . What? Come now, my good man." He said to the doctor, "It's a guest who says he doesn't like all those mice in his room." Then into the phone again: "Well, just pick out the mice you *do* like and we'll send the exterminator up for the rest. Thank *yum*." He hung the phone up before the doctor could pry it out of his hand. "This place is a madhouse. They say the nurses are striking. They're not as striking as some I've been out with, but they'll do. Ah, what have we here?"

The phone rang again almost instantly and this time the doctor got it. It was apparently the same caller, a baffled colleague to whom the situation was explained as briefly as possible. By the time the doctor had that bit of anarchy straightened out the patient had spotted Mrs. Swirling and sidled over, smiling amorously and flirting the cigar in his fingers.

"Haven't we met before? Don't tell me. Paris, Illinois. Rome, New York. No — Athens, Georgia! Am I close? Let me come a little closer." In lengthening his stride he stubbed his foot against the leg of a chair. "You must excuse me, I'm not myself today. I've just been in basket therapy and I'm still weaving."

"You do look familiar to me. And I must say you're acting it too, on rather short notice." She rose and circled off, putting her chair between them. "I think we met in transcendental meditation class. We had the same guru."

"Ah, yes, Bombay, New Delhi, strolls along the Ganges." Again he burst into song. "Way down upon the swami river, far, far away . . . !"

The doctor had finished his own conversation as swiftly as possible in order to follow the one going forward here. He observed the exchange sharply, taking in every detail, on the alert for some sign that the caller had by now recognized his quarry. There seemed to be none. He dished out the same surrealist patter he did with everyone else. But there was the one difference, that Mrs. Swirling could fall in with him by maneuvering in and out of remembered routines, as she jockeyed about among the furniture in order to keep a step or two ahead of her pursuer. The doctor also kept shifting his position so as to keep the two most advantageously in view. He looked at times like a baseball umpire monitoring a close play.

"I called on you in your room here a few times," Mrs. Swirling said. "Don't you remember?"

"Of course, of course. I'd like to see more of you. Will you be free Saturday?"

"I'm never free, and my rates go up weekends." Mrs. Swirling rested her weight on one very tidy hip and swung her bag by its strap as she popped an imaginary wad of gum. One could vividly picture the street lamppost behind her. "But maybe if you buy me lunch I'll think it over. I'm famished. What would you say to some moo goo gai pan?"

"I wouldn't say anything to it, I don't speak Chinese."

"Do you feel like a hamburger?"

"No, but maybe if I went out and got fried."

"I was hoping you'd join me in a cup of tea."

"Don't you think there'd be more room in a stein of beer?"

The doctor nodded solemn approval of the colloquy, the way it was going, particularly as to the manner in which Mrs. Swirling held up her end of it. But it bore little immediate therapeutic fruit. The gleam in Groucho Swirling's eye was tail light rather than love light, as he himself openly granted in a subsequent interview, for the good doctor to bowdlerize for any eventual psychiatric convention paper as best he could. There seemed to be not the least flicker of recognition, even after several more minutes of sprightly cross fire, and feeling no purpose could be served by prolonging the encounter, Dr. Josko signed for Mrs. Swirling to leave, in order that he might get on with his own procedures as planned. The patient loped alongside her to the door, hunched over so far his arms hung clear to his knees.

"I suppose you'd like me to call you a cab?"

"Yes, would you?"

"O.K., you're a cab. Now don't go turning into a side street. Goodbye! And more of this anon I trust." He munched some ladyfingers before letting her go, blowing her a kiss as she closed the door. "Now then, Doc, just what did you want to see me about?" He strode over to a bookshelf and took down a volume. "Hm. An anthology of the world's best thought."

"Feel free to borrow that if you'd like, Groucho. It's a popularization, but a good one. A sort of philosophical guide to living — and, for that matter, dying."

"Way to go, Doc! That's putting Descartes before de hearse." He clapped the book shut and squeezed it back in on the shelf. "I notice you carry a lot of weight around here, Doc."

"Thank you."

"Don't you think you ought to take a little of it off?"

"Well, you —"

"Look at those tires around your middle."

"You —"

"You're beginning to look like the Michelin Man."

"You —"

"You're getting so big I need double vision to take you in."

"You could do with a little reducing yourself. Not the Groucho I'd have recognized on the street. Ought to take advantage of our little gymnasium. Work out on the rowing machine, the parallel bars —"

"Parallel bars! One's enough for me. You must have me confused with W. C. Fields. My name is actually Goldwyn, and I wouldn't trust you with a ten-foot pole."

"Groucho, I'm curious."

"Let's face it, you're grotesque."

14

"No, I mean I'm curious *about* something. Something generally attributed to you. Possibly your most famous wisecrack. Did you really say you wouldn't belong to a club that would have you for a member?"

"Yeah, but I stole it from Henry James."

"?"

"In *The Princess Casamassima* the hero, what's-his-face, Hyacinth, tells somebody he'd never marry a girl who'd have him for a husband. Same gag."

The doctor paced the office, again thoughtfully kneading the underlip.

"Groucho. Groucho, I'd like to try something new today. There are so many blanks in your memory we ought to try to fill in. When did you first notice this amnesia?"

"I forget. I may have hit my head. We were having cocktails around a pool, and I fell in with drunken companions."

Dr. Josko pushed valiantly on, though feeling himself ever more helplessly sucked into a quagmire of surrealist slapstick in which he was doomed to play straight man, or "feed," as he seemed to remember such a foil was called. He turned and said abruptly: "I want to put you under hypnosis. You've been a good patient in many ways. Cooperative. I've got to give you credit."

"You might as well. I certainly can't pay cash."

"But first I'd like to give you a shot."

"Oh, good. I had you figured for the kind of Joe who keeps a bottle in his desk. I understand your hobby is music. Give you a diminished fifth anytime, eh, Doc? What drawer is it in? This one here?"

"No, no, no. Not that kind of shot. An injection. A sedative, just to quiet you down, make you more receptive to hypnotic suggestion. Would you take off your coat and roll up your sleeve, please?"

"Anything you say, Doc." He was remarkably amenable,

15

which the doctor chose to take as a faintly encouraging sign. The injection was administered in a moment.

"There you are. Thank you."

"Thank *yum*."

"Now, while we wait for it to take effect, you might tell me exactly what happened at the hospital. Where you were taken after that injury at the lawn benefit. You don't seem to remember, but you did a charity show, and you were quite good from what I'm told. Until you had that accident with your leg. From the hospital on your memory seems quite clear, so will you recall anything about that experience that comes to your mind?"

"Well, I was having my dinner in bed when the nurse came in, a nice ripe-looking redhead of about thirty-five. She was rather apologetic. 'Oh, I've come in to change your dressing,' she said. I said, 'That's not necessary. I got what I asked for, Thousand Island . . .' "

The submachine-gun crackle of gags continued until the doctor's head swam. He began to feel dizzy, as though he himself had taken the sedative. The patient all this while continued slouching and hunching about the room, poking into corners and picking up and fingering objects for derogatory comment. "I hocked a clock something like this once that turned out to be hot. They accused me of stealing it. Imagine! I was hauled down to the police station and told that anything I said might be held against me. So I said, 'Elizabeth Taylor.' But nothing ever came of it, and finally . . ."

Finally the sedative took effect, and the rambling, both oral and ambulatory, wound down.

"Now, why don't you just come over and lie down on this couch. That's fine. Stretch out and make yourself comfortable. Thank you."

"Thank *yum*."

"Now then. Speaking of timepieces, how do you like this

watch of mine? It's a Patek Philippe. A precious heirloom handed down from my great-grandfather." The doctor made a pendulum of it, swinging it slowly back and forth before the other's eyes. "Makes you drowsy, doesn't it? Fine. Just relax. Go to sleep. Don't fight it . . . Good . . . Now I want you to tell me exactly. . ."

The Principal Themes

Two

IT ALL BEGAN with a misunderstanding. Swirling was going through the drawers of his wife's desk looking for an airmail envelope when he came across some pages in her handwriting that first aroused his curiosity, and then finally, as their contents dawned on him, struck him forcibly as nothing less than a eulogy, or at least some rough notes for a eulogy, to be delivered over his remains in the foreseeable future. His eyes bulged, and his lips pursed in a low whistle of amazement. There was certainly no mistaking the elegiac note struck by such passages as, "We are all on loan to one another, to be foreclosed who knows when . . . this short day of frost and sun, as Walter Pater calls our lives . . . Kalamazoo . . . If he suspected how serious his condition was, he never . . . sparing us that to the very . . . courage an example to all of us."

"Good God," Swirling exclaimed as he clapped the drawer shut and a hand to his brow, as though the sound of his own voice might dispel the specter he had unleashed. He did not want to be an example of courage at all — at least not quite yet. Even were he cast in that mold. So then it was Enid, his wife, who was never "letting on," concealing from him what the doctor must have confided to her but kept from his patient (Swirling had thought himself in the clear after some recent tests).

The conclusions to which he jumped were perfectly understandable in the circumstances. The word *Kalamazoo*, leaping off the page at him, was as responsible as the commemorative prose for the muddle into which he had been plunged. What he had happened on was simply a letter of condolence Enid was writing to the widow of a friend, Fred Sharkey, who, by one of those coincidences out of which Fate brews some of her wickeder confusions, had been born and raised in Kalamazoo about the same time as Swirling himself, though their paths had never crossed there. Swirling naturally figured that the references to his hometown were to be part of a brief biographical sketch of the sort that are generally woven into tributes read at funeral services, or incorporated in memorial pamphlets, or both.

Making rather wildly for the liquor cabinet, he wondered how long he had, according to consultations now to be seen in hindsight as having been conducted behind his back. The time-honored six months to a year? As he poured himself a stiff belt of bourbon he seemed to remember a certain ... well, yes, evasiveness in Enid's manner every time the subject of his complaint had come up, or the tests had been discussed. Or was he imagining all that? He hadn't imagined a couple of unexplained phone calls she'd made on the extension in that very study, and reported on only in the vaguest mumbles later. All this was to be understood in perspective as part of the protective hugger-mugger between doctor and — he did not flinch at the term — widow-elect.

He stood at the window gulping from his glass as a

scenario unreeled in his mind, one that must include a valedictory visit to old Kazoo. Once more to call on those comi-
cally celebrated but to him beloved celery fields, where as a
boy he had worked in summertimes to augment the meager
family income . . . Three months? Less, in all probability, if
wheels must already be set in motion for the "arrange-
ments." It must be a poor prognosis indeed that would start a
devoted but nothing-if-not-realistic wife to work on a tribute
better guaranteeing the deceased his due than if left at the
last minute to the blind actualities of bereavement. All that
he quite understood — enough to applaud its practicality. To
applaud, even, its calculation. Oh, he could imagine the
unimaginative taking exception if they knew, being captious
about it. "Couldn't wait to . . ." Nonsense. He had attended
some hurry-up jobs in his day, those overnight paste-ups of
inspirational claptrap from Tennyson and Wordsworth, the
tired old Twenty-third Psalm, and a prayer or two thrown in
by a minister into whose lap the whole thing had had to be
dumped because the immediate family were running around
like chickens with their heads cut off. No such slapdash
obsequies were to be Bob Swirling's lot. He was to be credit-
ably put by, it would appear. Nothing less would do with
stouthearted Enid taking hold so well in advance! Even now
he could see her — this very minute tearfully trundling a cart
through the supermarket as she mentally revolved new material or polished the draft he'd glimpsed, phrases suited to the
occasion and worthy of the subject. "Never a whimper of
self-concern . . . that eagle heart . . ."

She was what used to be called a brick, Enid. Always the
sort who got the damn thing done right, when faced with a
job of work. Hell, she'd written the very wedding ceremony
they'd started life off with, sweeping away all that moldy
Pauline malarkey about the wife obeying and such, and
hammering out instead a no-nonsense covenant between
equals entering a by now rickety institution in what was

23

probably one of the worst of all possible worlds. Kazoo all forgot, Swirling smiled at the memory of the justice of the peace they'd knocked up one night (Enid was half English) in Virginia, reading the marriage form handed him on a sheet of paper, and at the memory of the justice's wife standing by as a witness in a flannel bathrobe, just like in the movies, giving a sniff of Pauline censorship at the blasphemous contract before padding back to bed again. Swirling had then been given leave to kiss the bride already some twenty times ravished, and as he did so the wife's slippers slapped out a recessional on the bare oak floor. Somewhere in this house was that marriage form, written in the bride's strong, flowing hand. And now she was drafting a farewell encomium to the groom.

He sprinted back to the liquor cabinet. Replenished glass at lip, he struggled with the temptation to go back into the study. Resuming the search for the airmail envelope, temporarily driven out of his mind, would be an excuse — though it smacked of subterfuge. After a moment's hesitation he set his glass down, went back and slid the drawer furtively open again. From a standing position, he queasily rolled an eye downward at the manuscript. It was in pencil on a block of the ruled yellow legal-size paper on which Enid liked to compose communications of any kind. How often he had seen her, as they sat together in the evening lamplight, with a pad of it propped on her knee as she drafted a letter to her Congressman, or a flaming manifesto for one or another of the ecological causes into which she threw herself, and sometimes him.

Swirling tried to recover the sense of happenstance in which he had first stumbled on the fateful document, so as to make it again something that had "accidentally caught his eye." He even pretended he was still looking for the airmail envelope.

". . . capacity for friendship we shall all of us always miss," swam into focus. Well, he could lay claim to that attribute without undue complacency. Why not? What else? Gingerly he turned the top page halfway back, curling it upward from the bottom. There were several lines heavily deleted, followed by a presumably refined version of what must be said. "Those who knew and loved him will always remember his perennial good humor, wry but never unkind, tart but never caustic." He nodded, choking back his emotion. Yes, he trusted that also answered to the case. ". . . open and unstinting generosity for the loss of which we are all the poorer . . ." Quite, quite, he was the poorer himself for all the tens and twenties he had shelled out to wastrels a little short till Saturday. "The stoic calm with which he faced the end —"

The force with which he slammed the drawer shut was like a pistol shot. Stoic calm indeed — on *her* part! And who would read all this from the pulpit? Probably Dick Pilbeam, pastor of the catchall Unitarian church on which the unaffiliated all threw themselves for nuptial and thanatopsical events. What a hell of a thing to have stumbled on! Christ, it was like eavesdropping on your own funeral, like Tom Sawyer and Huckleberry Finn. He forgave a thousand writers that moth-eaten "as if in a dream" cliché, which quite described his sensation as he wandered about, glass in hand. He caught a glimpse of his face in a wall mirror, and paused to take it in. It was weirdly unfamiliar, the face of a stranger. He felt already "departed." He had once heard of an industrialist, an oil magnate or something on the tycoon level, who had been shown his obituary by a well-meaning friend, a reporter who helped stockpile such obits for a metropolitan daily, and been so overcome as nearly to have required its being rushed into print for the morning edition. But he had survived the preview by a good twenty years. "I'll beat this rap too," Swirling said aloud. The successive fast whiskeys released floods of emotion similar, no doubt, to those that had all but felled the petroleum king untimely. Astonishment, excitement, a kind of elation even, boiled together with fear and courage, affection and, yes, self-pity, like eddies in a riptide. He had never seen a whole hell of a lot wrong with feeling sorry for yourself. If you don't, who will?

Well, maybe that wasn't altogether true. Hadn't the greetings of his friends been a little warmer lately, their parting handclasps a bit more heartfelt? They all probably *knew*. Otherwise why had Charlie Tingle given him his first edition of *The Grapes of Wrath* at that fortieth birthday party Steve Baldridge had thrown for him the week before? Or Steve, who normally poured his guests Gallo and Mission Bell, broken out his vintage Burgundies? Swirling remembered thinking at the time *Charlie Tingle* might have been given six months to a year, and was seeing to the dispersal of his treasures into more deserving hands than those of his ex-wife, Becky, one of those women you don't give a book because they've already got one. No, that was unfair. He took that back. She was a pretty parcel over whom he had salivated aplenty. But in any case, the circumstances apparently made Enid the ultimate recipient of the Steinbeck. No, he wasn't imagining things in retrospect. They were all probably already mentally polishing up their expressions of condolence, for the stack of letters he could visualize accumulating on Enid's desk after the hour had struck. And into their replies would go the same painstaking care she was giving the biographical sketch cum paean that was to be read by Dick Pilbeam, or to be bound and distributed as a memorial pamphlet, or both. Swirling could see that little commemorative booklet clearly too. Something done in handsomely tasteful type, on deckle-edge paper, with a tasseled cord running through the spine, like those menus in larcenous restaurants.

Well so. A measure of self-commiseration was all right, but one mustn't wallow in it. No. One must pull oneself together and get down to practicalities, like Enid herself. (She would let go later.) One thing he had so far failed to do was make clear his preference as to, duh, er, means of disposal. No embarrassment of riches there! The prospect of burial is hardly palatable to anyone with any instinct for self-preservation, while the mere thought of cremation turned him ashen. Good God, what was he saying? Thought of cremation turned him, oh, that was rich. Never mind that now, he could drop the definitive hint later, or simply tell his lawyer, maybe after flipping a coin. What did it really matter? What mattered was easing the task on which Enid was bent and embarked, relative to what was to be read or printed (or both). Here favorite poets of the deceased's were always a great help. In fact quotations from any source at all that had "helped him along life's way" were valuable things with which to stud funerary appreciations, as their almost universal use attested. Enid herself had already tucked in the phrase from Walter Pater, though Swirling had never read him. Her fondness for him probably dated back to the college term paper she'd done on him. Swirling vividly recalled how effective had been a quotation from Edna Millay in a service he had recently attended, for poor dear Monica Tetley. What poem had it been from again? "Dirge Without Music" if memory served. He found it readily enough in an anthology plucked off the shelf, and read it aloud, with feeling:

Into the darkness they go, the wise and the lovely. Crowned
With lilies and laurel they go; but I am not resigned.

Quietly they go, the intelligent, the witty, the brave.
I know. But I do not approve. And I am not resigned.

So overcome was he with the sentiment expressed in the lines that he broke down as he read them. He fairly shook with simple, unabashed emotion. Until he suddenly remembered something. He couldn't stand Edna St. Vincent Millay. Never had. He had taken an early scunner to that schoolgirl

27

gush. But what had really finished him off was seeing her poetry *danced,* at a performance to which he had been dragged like a tired businessman halfway across Connecticut. In the stress of the moment it had completely slipped his mind that she wasn't his dish of tea — any more than Enid's, if it came to that. He wiped his eyes, blew his nose, and put the anthology away again.

What *were* some "lines" that had made a great impression on him, and concerning which he might drop hints? All he could think of was one from Edwin Arlington Robinson, that for some reason was stuck in his memory like a post in cement. "Never build a stairway for a swallow." He couldn't even recall the poem it was from, much less what it meant. Probably from one of the book-length works he'd been required to read in college. He intoned the line aloud now, then added, finger aloft, "That's advice I have always heeded, and never lived to regret." Hey, what about delivering his own farewell while he was still alive, by God and by Jesus, a sort of surrealist ceremony to which he would invite all his friends — he must be getting stewed now — a small gem of self-belittlement that would have them scarcely knowing whether they were laughing or crying as they rolled in the aisles unfurling handkerchiefs of their own. The bit of a minute ago about how the very thought of cremation turned him ashen, that should be good for a laugh, even at ovenside, let alone for this feast he would throw. Of course it had been unconscious, but even so. He could work in some of his Groucho stuff. He tried a little aloud now. "My doctor gave me six months to live. You can imagine I didn't like that, so I went to another doctor, and he gave me six months. That gave me a year right there. I went to a third, and after a thorough examination he gave me eighteen months. That gives me a total of two and a half years so far. I figure I need about three years to wind up my affairs, and, brother, are they affairs . . ." Yes, he could see them all, Charlie Tingle and

28

Steve and Ethel Baldridge, and especially little Becky Tingle, whose eyes misted over at the slightest provocation, moved to tears of grateful laughter at this spectacle of heroism without heroics, of an, oh, an easy, undeluded elegance of spirit, a throwaway grace that nevertheless had a kind of divinity in it.

"I wish no memorial service of any kind to be held for me." He said that aloud, to clear the air. Because he was really getting into his cups and must take firm hold of himself before Enid got back from her shopping. He did pour himself a last tiny one, though, this time on the rocks, and as he watched the liquor trickle over the ice cubes, he stroked his neatly trimmed mustache with the ball of one finger. Music. What about musical selections? Standard organ backgrounds supplied by morticians not otherwise instructed were depressing; canned treacle seeping through louvers was the worst. "Over my dead body," he stoutly declared. But what would, just as a matter of interest, be appropriate? Enid knew perfectly well his tastes, no coaching necessary there. Debussy and Ravel, and possibly a good two-thirds of Stravinsky. She no doubt remembered his saying that if there were one recording he could take to the proverbial desert island (presupposing a coconut palm with an electric socket in its trunk into which a stereo could be plugged) it would be the *Daphnis and Chloë*. He never tired of its suavely luscious harmonics. Oh, and Scriabin, slowly but surely coming into his own as a major composer. Mustn't forget the *Poem of Ecstasy,* a recent addiction. Its trumpeted eloquences might well purge the atmosphere right here and now! He would put his Dimitri Mitropoulos LP on.

He was digging it out of the rack where he kept his albums when he heard the crunch of tires on the gravel drive outside. From a window he saw, not one, but two cars pull into the yard. Behind their yellow station wagon, from which

29

Enid was emerging with a sack of groceries, a red Volkswagen drew to a stop. Becky Tingle climbed out of that, laughing and calling something over to Enid as she clapped the door shut. The two had obviously met at the supermarket and Becky had been invited to stop in for a drink — or more likely invited herself — on her way home. No novelty that, as Enid was famous for the continual round of klatschers dropping in for that purpose, or for coffee in the midmornings. The informed wit of her gossip and the educated intelligence of her small talk made her attractive to women who, themselves, might have nothing better to do than chatter the idle hours away — anything but true of Enid. Many of the perennially changing circle of klatschers were subtly recruited for her political and civic causes. Most of them gave more than they took in the way of local dirt, Enid being instinctively appreciated and prized as a confidante who could be trusted not to betray secrets recognized as such, and not intended for further disbursement to other klatschers. But she mistrusted people who "never gossiped" as lacking in the normal human curiosity about their fellows. Swirling expected Becky was here to unload about her recent divorce, though that wasn't why he made himself scarce.

He hesitated irresolutely in the front vestibule, torn between empirical boredom with Becky's conversation and enchantment with her face and figure. Then he bolted up the stairs two at a time at the last split second before the door opened and Becky was heard to say, "— name actually is Carpool."

Swirling lay stretched out on the bed and put his house in order.

On his own desk was the current issue of the Authors Guild Bulletin, which featured an article stressing the importance of specifying a literary executor, to help spare one's heirs and assigns the gruesome snarls of probate. Entanglement in tax and monetary problems was something to which Swirling had long aspired, rather than anything he feared. There would be nothing for his literary executor to do but throw out the hundred or so pages of an abandoned novel. Mrs. Bokum, their cleaning woman, had very nearly already done so, thus putting him in a class with Carlyle, whose manuscript of *The French Revolution* a servant had used to light a fire. Speaking of fires, Swirling could remember to the hour — in fact to the exact minute — when his own had gone out.

It was a bright Saturday afternoon in midsummer. He was watching a polo match at the Chichester Country Club, one he frequented as an authority on the sport, not to say its ranking buff. It was one of the subjects on which he hammered out feature articles for sports magazines and the Sunday supplement sections of metropolitan dailies. On the sacred principle of Writing About What You Know, he was laying his novel in that narrow but exciting world. *Saturday Thunder* took its title from the ravishing sound of the horses' hooves as they pounded down the field, lashed by riders themselves driven by the demons that make us press on for the sexual and social trophies as well as the athletic and professional, gladiators as sick for the admiration of the expensive sun-bronzed women watching from the stands as for the gold cup awaiting the victor at the end of his cavalry charges.

He was now these hundred pages into the book when he learned something virtually by accident. Filling in with some incidental commentary, the announcer was saying, "Contrary to what the public or the superficial observer might think, or assume, the ball is not struck with the end of the mallet, as in croquet, but the side."

Swirling sat in open-mouthed disbelief for fully a minute, stunned, oblivious to whatever else followed this revelation over the public-address system. Then he pocketed his pencil and note pad, rose, and picked his way to the clubhouse. Slumped over a drink at the bar, he shook his head in dazed incredulity. Eight years of writing about polo, known for half of them as the country's leading devotee, "at work on a novel about the inside world of the sport," as the notes on contributors said in the magazines in which his pieces appeared, and he hadn't known you smacked the old apple with the side of the hammer, not the nose. *He had observed nothing.* God alone knew what else he watched in this world without seeing a thing.

As if in a dream, he turned and looked over his shoulder at the clock on the wall. Three-fifteen. Allowing for five minutes in which to slink out of the stands toward the bar and arm himself with the glass around which his nerveless fingers now coldly curved, he could pinpoint his moment of truth as 3:10 P.M. on Saturday, August the twenty-second. From that moment the dream lay dead inside him, a clinker. And, dead, he might as well embalm himself in double bourbons. He could just faintly hear the announcer rubbing salt into his wounds. "Another thing the uninitiated might be ignorant of is that the shaft is set into the mallet at a slant, not a right angle at all, in order to compensate for the rider's own angle in relation to —" Swirling put his fingers in his ears, but sentences he had written himself buzzed in his head like a swarm of hornets he could not shoo away or ever again in his lifetime elude. "To Ferdie van Rensselaer no thrill on earth could compare to the electric charge that ran through the stem of the mallet and up your every nerve and muscle as you felt the nose of the hammer hit the ball square in a clean shot through the goal . . . McElroy might ridicule the game as mounted croquet, but if that tippling wag could once experience the ecstasy of wheeling your mount with one hand while with the other you swung your gavel in a perfect arc to connect the back or front of the hammer smack with a still-rolling ball ... Delacroix horsemen writhing in and out of melees with their weapons flailing ..."

"What's the matter, mister, something the matter?"

"No, I'm all right."

"You were shaking your head. And your ears hurt?"

"No, no. I'll have another."

Delacroix horsemen had been good mock purple, and the gavel was a nice throwaway too, but with how many other errors of fact mightn't the stuff be riddled? Not that he wasn't grateful for being dealt this shock before it was too late. Published, he would have been ten times the fool. It was unlikely that he would have drawn an editor familiar enough with polo to catch the boo-boos, which would then almost certainly slip past the copy department, to reach at last the light of day. My God, he would have been a laughingstock. He would have wanted to kill himself under the flood of those letters readers take a gleeful pleasure in writing. He had written his own share. Those crows flapping home to roost would have blackened the sky like the Crucifixion itself.

Not that there hadn't been portents, forewarnings that he lacked the powers of observation essential to the novelist. In the gibble-gabble of a dinner party one time, Ed Cogshell had undertaken to correct a factual error in the Praxiteles statue of Hercules standing in the Louvre. "He's got the left testicle the lower of the two. That's wrong. It's the right that's the lower."

"No it isn't," Charlie Tingle had piped up. "Mine isn't. Mine's the left."

A controversy had ensued — it was over brandies and the ladies had been shepherded off by the hostess — during which notes were compared and testimonies given. With the interesting fact emerging that the phenomenon varied. It could be one or the other, as one can be right-handed or left.

Three testified to the left, with Hercules — or Praxiteles — three to the right. Tied at three all. Swirling hadn't yet voted. It was up to him to break the tie.

"Bob? What do you say?" This from Cogshell as host. "Bob?"

He didn't know. He had no idea. He literally could not answer without research. So he'd just said, "Right," a lucky stab as it turned out on later scrutiny. Because in all his forty years he had observed nothing. Not even about himself. Not even at such times, to be regarded as permissibly narcissistic, when one stood for a few moments before a full-length mirror to drink oneself in.

The host began pulling art books down from the shelves and spreading them open on the coffee table. "Michelangelo has the Dying Slave's on the right. That's in the Louvre too. In the one called the Demon he ducks it. Let's see his David ... Oh, this illustration only shows the upper half. What about the Rodin book. Ed? That show anything?"

The ladies filed back in.

"Well, well, what are you boys up to? Quite a cultural evening going on here. Bob, what are you and Tubby fidgeting with yourselves about?"

That would leave only the stoutly unproduced play for the literary executor to chuck out — if he could find it. Where was *Mrs. Locksley's Flesh* anyway? Probably still gathering dust in the office of the one producer who'd shown a flicker of interest, and that merely enough to show it to an established playwright in hopes of a collaboration — of which nothing had ever come. But he must remind Enid of his remark about that. "He's looking for somebody to adapt my play to the stage." That should be worth a laugh at ovenside, one illustrating the deceased's healing humor, a clear-eyed modesty still bracing to one and all in loving memory. Coupled with it might be his notion that that famous fell sergeant who is so strict in his arrest must, in fact, if Shakespeare is not to be charged with mixed metaphor, be a cop. To whom Swirling was quite ready to say, "I'll go quietly, officer."

He was smiling ruefully at these musings when the door opened almost noiselessly and Enid put her impressive red head in.

"Asleep?"

"Rather doubt it."

She came all the way in, swinging the door to without shutting it. "Becky Tingle's here," she said, rolling her eyes in not altogether mock distraction. "Want to come down? This may be the day when she'll finish a sentence. You wouldn't want to miss that first, would you?"

"Guess not." He sat up and swung his legs over the side of the bed.

Becky's rhapsodically disjointed delivery was proverbial among their friends, many of whom decided that Charlie had called it quits and got a divorce because he simply couldn't stand any more of waiting for the other syntactical shoe to drop. Enid had gone so far as to imagine the scene that had finally split the Tingle household in two.

"What does Nora Tetzel give you that I don't?"

"Predicates!"

Having padded silently down the carpeted stairway, Swirling paused on the bottom step to eavesdrop a moment on the women, again stroking his pencil-thin mustache with a fingertip as he listened. They were talking houses, which in Becky's case was talking shop. She had gone into real estate brokerage after the breakup of her marriage, and was now describing a property about to be thrown on the market for which every agency wanted the exclusive. It was Enid's part of the discussion that Swirling found significant; it indicated again that she was looking for something to buy with a little inherited money of her own, and then put up for rent. As a widow, she could use the money when what little he had to leave her was used up. Mainly the thirty-five thousand dollars' worth of insurance which comprised the bulk of his estate. Thank God he had boosted it from fifteen.

"Seven rooms, with a studio living room that — it absolutely soars to these clerestory windows, with these handsome stained — and a skylight in the middle. The owner's been transferred to what. Brussels and has to unload. It's, I'll tell you, it's sort of nestled in — you know that dogleg in Benson Road just below the Mills farm?"

"Ah ha."

"Shall I keep you posted the minute I —?"

"Well, actually I've talked to ..." Here the sound of a kitchen match struck on the corrugated cup of an ashtray indicated that Enid had paused to light one of her elegant cigars. Time out till it was got going. "I asked Helen Tarbell to keep an eye out for me, so I guess it wouldn't be cricket."

"Oh, of course. Helen's a good agent, but, um, do stop and peek in the window anytime. It's empty now. But anybody with some ready — I'd say about ninety-five five will be the asking, and any bank would be glad to — You'd get six hundred a month for it easy. But put Helen on the qui vive. It'll be snapped up like that."

"Ah ha. Well, thanks a lot, Becky. Real estate is always the best investment."

"Especially in this part of Connecticut. I haven't nearly the wherewithal or — Oh, what I meant to say about rent. When you figure I pay Mrs. Pesky two hundred and fifty for that dinky apartment. Of course it's furnished ..."

Through his fingertips Swirling was reminded of a nagging problem: whether he would have to shave his mustache off in order to put on the greasepaint one he'd need to do the Groucho at his do-it-yourself obsequies, or the charity benefit he had promised to emcee, if he lived that long. He was sandy-haired, and it would probably show through. He was working up a few more zingers for delivery at ovenside when there was a break in the conversation as Enid went to freshen Becky's drink. Swirling walked in.

"Hello, hello, hello!"

"Well, look who's. How are you, Bobby? You're looking simply terrific."

Too much emphasis. And the smile excessively prolonged. Dead giveaway. He must look a shadow of his former self. The Enemy already deeply entrenched in his vitals. They all knew. So he must put up as good a front himself. Up, my feathers! No, that was more Millay!

When he circled a coffee table, bumping it with his leg, to shake Becky's extended hand, she drew him downward and put her face up to be pecked, and not necessarily on the cheek, so that he sustained a crimson smudge on one lip. Suspecting as much, he furtively swiped a hand across it while turning his back to make for a chair. He had once divided his and Enid's women friends into two categories, then asked Enid to guess on what basis he had sorted them out. Giving up, she had been told: those who present the cheek, and those who mouth-smack, on being greeted. The game had then gone on in terms of testing his classification as a key to personality; whether it distinguished the uptight from the spontaneous, the conventional from known or suspected swingers, etc. That had not washed. What had thrown the criterion off was the continental double-bussers, the rapidly spreading jet-age breed who kiss you first on one cheek and then the other, with an accompanying bear hug — as though one were being decorated by a head of state.

Becky brought her two hands together. "I must tell you about my class! At Back to School? The new continuing education center?"

"Ah ha," Enid said as she brought Becky's replenished highball.

Swirling turned down the thermostat of his attention to the

bare minimum required for following the conversation in case he was asked a question or required to make a response, while inwardly pursuing an entirely separate and unrelated line of thought.

The blow dealt him at the polo match, with its accompanying larger deflations, had made the question of his powers of observation not just a sore point but a positive obsession. He put them to the test everywhere, to prove that his humiliation had been a fluke, a one-shot shortcoming, and that he not only looked, but saw. Or to tighten the distinction to the Sherlock Holmes level, he not only saw, but observed. And one of the phenomena he noticed was that the testicles thing had its counterpart in women's breasts. One of those was generally lower than the other also. Or higher, if you preferred to think of it that way. The facts could be freely enough researched, God knew, in this permissive day! In erotic movie and stage scenes; on the covers of nude magazines everywhere festooning newsstands; even on the street with all those brassiereless women striding toward you. Becky Tingle's breasts were small but shapely, and apple-hard you knew. And since now she obviously wore nothing under a blouse itself translucent, he could plainly add to his present statistical total — of 37 lower for the right, 11 for the left — another for the right. That seemed to be the one normally lower, then. A carpenter's level held to Becky's person would have found perhaps a quarter of an inch difference in the height at which the rosebud tips tantalizingly embossed the taut yellow pullover, and her posture as she sat with her arms outspread along the back of the couch made it necessary for Swirling to will his gaze elsewhere, even as in spirit he fondled and tasted, first the one, then the other of those dumplings. A mad thought inflamed an already checkered afternoon: that a man under sentence of death had a right, not only to entertain such fantasies, but to hope he might act on them as well, while life and breath remained.

Time's wingèd chariot was validly invoked to warn even the normally living to gather rosebuds while they might; how much more so in the case of one for whom that chariot is now already swinging low, indeed taxiing toward him on the runway, coming for to carry him home. It was not later than *he* thought. He knew what time it was! *Was* Becky privy to his plight? Would it have weighed in her reckoning? At parties, they had often eye-flirted, holding each other's glances in a way that, for her part, might mean a good deal or nothing at all. The ego grazes in odd ways and unexpected pastures, and sexual speculation, simply as such, makes for a lot of coquettes with nothing more on their minds than having their vanity tickled. Still, one could never tell. She must know her effect on him right this minute.

"Do I dare to eat a peach?"

"Uh, what did you say, Becky?"

"That's the line Dick Rubber threw out when our class — oh, it's not a class, just a group — broke up last time. Is it poetry? That's the assignment for this week. Something for us to think about. And decide, each in his own heart."

Swirling assembled into a coherent pattern what his ears had half caught in the past five minutes. Becky attended a weekly session labeled, in the Back to School catalogue, "We Moderns," a free-for-all seminar in contemporary literature run by one Dick Rubber. In this case the returnees, as those going back to school were called, had little or no knowledge of the subject — they were just partially educated people in the market solely for intellectual stimulation, with no interest in formal credit. Dick Rubber had sent his charges off with that provocative question, for them to mull and decide about in the week's interval till next time.

"So?" Becky shrugged and gave a self-belittling laugh. "Is it poetry?"

"It better be. It's from Eliot," Enid said. She lounged in a deep chair, her long legs sheathed in orange slacks, her ankles crossed on an ottoman, drawing on a cigar thinner than a panatela, from which a precarious inch of ash threatened to drop down her black scoop-necked blouse. Mesmerized, they watched her take still another deep drag before tapping it into an ashtray she held in her lap. Enid's cigars somehow enhanced a naturally aristocratic bearing, besides emphasizing her independence. "'The Love Song of J. Alfred Prufrock' is full of those prosaic lines, like, let's see, it's so long since I've read it. 'I have measured out my life with coffee spoons.' I guess that's what your teacher wants to get a discussion going about — can a flat statement be poetry. Eliot would be good pickin's for that. 'The nightingales are singing near the Convent of the Sacred Heart' is a factual statement — of piercing beauty."

"She should be teaching it." Becky made a gesture recommending Swirling's wife to him, wagging a thumb in her direction.

"Somehow these prosaic notes come out song in Eliot. I don't read poetry anymore because what I miss in what I do come across today is the sense of song. I want to be picked up and deposited elsewhere, preferably somewhere I've never been. All this lint picking and eyebrow combing. The poet's own hemidemisemiquavers about nothing much. I guess I shouldn't judge. But my recollection is, that's the sort of thing Eliot is satirizing in 'Prufrock,' in a way. This sort of dehydrated aesthete, too fastidious to live. He'd probably get menopause if he did dare to eat a peach. Hey, Bob." Enid slid erect in her chair. "Come to think of it, that's what Harriet Boyle, remember her, my college roommate, that's exactly the line she asked Eliot about in a question period after a reading in New York. Eliot told her what he'd had in mind when he wrote the line, and she said it had always meant something completely different to her, and told him. Eliot laughed and said that was all right with him too."

"What did he say it meant? Oh, what did he say it meant?" Becky asked, clapping her hands together.

"I don't remember. Or what my friend thought either."

"Could you call her and ask her? It's the sort of thing the class — and it would bowl Dick Rubber over."

"She's dead."

"Damn."

Becky drank from her highball, holding it in both hands, like a child drinking its milk. Shifting his eyes toward Enid, Swirling saw that she had been watching him watch Becky. Becky herself seemed to catch a certain self-conscious vibration pass between the other two, or at least so Swirling imagined. He didn't, now, imagine the undertone of resentment with which Becky defended her enrollment in the Back to School extension-course center, whose substitution of spontaneous rambling for disciplined study Enid called rumpus room education. He remembered something Enid had once said about Becky's prickliness when differed with. It was Enid's theory that the aggressiveness proverbially associated with limited stature was truer of women than of men. "The worst Napoleons are women," she said, "just as the worst bitches are men. I worked for two bantam hens, and I know what it's like."

"There are many kinds of learning, you know," Becky said, "and people who don't have time for, or aren't interested in credits per se — what's the difference whether you're talking about Yeats one minute and Jung the next, or how the ball bounces, as long as people come *away* with something. Or the poetry class gets mixed up with an encounter group wandering into the wrong room. Oh, it's hard to explain Dick's freewheeling method. You'd have to see it in, hey, why don't you two guys come. Students are allowed to take guests. It's Tuesday evenings."

"There's that town meeting about saving the wetlands

then," Enid said. "From that paper company that wants to put up a factory. Spew the Sound with every known chemical. But you go, Bob, if you'd like. I'll raise enough hell for the whole family. You can tell me what came of the peach bit."

"Well, I'll see," Swirling said.

Becky drained her glass and shouldered her bag. "Got to run. I want you two to come to dinner as soon as I get settled. Got a new recipe for bouillabaisse. Everything goes into it except bits and pieces of the Loch Ness monster." They followed her to the door. "It's Tuesdays at eight, Bob, if you find yourself in the mood. At the old Trumbull school, you know?"

The Swirlings stood on the front stoop watching Becky maneuver her Volkswagen out of the drive without too much damage to the shrubbery. She waved as she made off in a spray of gravel. Enid pitched her cigar stub into the bushes and led the way in. After closing the door she leaned her head back against it, like an actress in a film. Her great brown eyes rolled like a pair of marbles in Swirling's direction.

"Jesus. I always feel physically disheveled after an hour with that one. My hair needs combing, my clothes pressing. Bouillabaisse is right for her. That's what her head is — a great bubbling fish stew. Everything in it *including* bits and pieces of the Loch Ness monster." Her smile became good-naturedly teasing, as though she were picking up from the moment she'd caught him drooling over the subject. "It's probably your view that she's scatterbrained, but not from the neck down. Right? Won't that be your story?"

"Right. But remember you said it, and I'm not the first bloke to think it. Don't worry, though, she doesn't have your figure. You're marmoreal, hey."

"What does that mean?"

"Look it up."

Three

SO ENID WAS SUBTLY but surely giving him leave to enjoy himself in any quarter for which he might have the taste or inclination, while time remained. That was how Swirling read the signals being flashed him. He would be indulged in whatever manner he had a will for, till his curtain came down. She had always been reasonable, but this! To as much as convey her compliance beforehand — even put the bee in his bonnet — that was largeheartedness for which a man could be truly thankful. Yet there it was, the dispensation, handed him on a platter of sly innuendo. To enjoy heartily what he must leave 'ere long — or however Shakespeare put it. He was like a monk given his misericorde — that lovely word for an indulgence granted in a monastery, such as the relaxation of a rule for fasting. That theirs was an avowedly open marriage from which Enid herself was suspected to have wandered in a tryst or two hardly figured; it did not qualify her generosity or lessen his gratitude. He remembered the old hymn in which they had so often raised their voices in the church at Kalamazoo — "Work, for the night is coming." He was to be let play till it did.

It was in the spirit of that delicately discreet, that almost ethereally civilized understanding that he did indeed act on the invitation to be a guest at "We Moderns."

The wall thermometer nestled in the cleft of Becky Tingle's bosom was a costume pendant hanging from a silver chain around her neck, and the mercury tube running its length was flanked by numbered notches that gave the temperature in both Fahrenheit readings and the threatened Celsius system. The classroom was a cool sixty degrees and mustily damp, and atmospheric discomfort was compounded by cramped seating accommodations. The Adult Education and Arts Center was housed in a long-abandoned elementary school building, equipped with nostalgic desk-chair combinations. Most of the women in the group sat sidesaddle, with their legs in the aisle, but the men, Swirling included, wedged their knees in under the desk, as though more fully to recover the sense of being schoolboys once again.

Feeling gingerly about in his desk compartment, wary of decomposed apple cores, pellets of chewing gum, mouse skeletons and other memorabilia of long-ago occupancy by ten o'clock scholars, Swirling found only an old ruler, with which he fiddled as he smiled nervously across the aisle at Becky. It broke in two as he did so. She had been in her seat when he arrived, unmistakably watching the door, and had given a gasp of pleasure at his materialization. She beckoned him over and patted the seat next to hers, which she had been saving. He squeezed in under the desk, grinding his knees on its underside until he had managed to settle his forelegs on a slant. A certain flushed embarrassment at their being together, in what seemed already a tryst uneasily prophetic of guilt to come, heightened his going-back-to-school sensation, with its overtones of early mischief. As though he were a truant *in* school, playing hooky from home there. As though another time, sitting behind her in whispered delinquency and chewing his own gum on the sly, he would dip her braids into his inkwell to conceal his terrible desire to carry her books home when the three-o'clock bell sounded deliverance. There actually were inkwells in the desks and Becky did have her hair in braids, but the inkwells were dry and the braids were crossed to form a tiara on the top of her head. Gave her a little more height.

Taking stock of the other five members of the "appreciation workshop," as it was called, as though the grasp of literature was a matter of unremitting toil rather than an aesthetic pleasure, Swirling recognized his butcher, Burt Winkleheart, who waved across the room in greeting. He flittered his fingers like Oliver Hardy, as though to exhibit and declare their astonishing resemblance to pork sausages. He was an inveterate taker of extension courses, on the principle that it was never too late to learn, and also that he might talk about something other than meat with his educated customers. It was they who were put to it to hold up their end of a conversation initiated by Winkleheart. Swirling had learned in the course of a few weeks' purchases alone that Van Gogh didn't actually cut off his ear, only the lobe of it; that if the Saracens hadn't been defeated in the battle of Tours in 732 we would all be Moslems instead of Christians; and that plovers not only ride the backs of crocodiles but enter their mouths in order to pick their teeth. Near Winkleheart were a pair of eighteen-year-old twin sisters, dressed alike, all right enough, but not in matching store "outfits." They wore blue jeans into the flanks and seat of which incidental oddments such as daisies, war cries and arcane insignia were sewn, soiled sneakers and unpressed denim shirts — all in keeping with the antibourgeois mode of the hour. Swirling, who had seen them often, always felt that their collaged persons were a manifesto aimed at him as a

45

bathed and groomed homeowner with a Sno Blower in the garage, but he nevertheless found the two irresistibly charming as they swung along the street together, dressed alike as things of shreds and patches. Better got up but far less prepossessing was a man named Carswell, unmasked as a local detective with ambitions to write novels like those of Raymond Chandler. He was taking a course in composition, also taught by Dick Rubber, but figured a little extra bloom rubbed off on him here wouldn't hurt. He puffed a large cigar, the smoke from which Mrs. Lapidus, who sat in front of him, kept waving away with reproachful gestures and punitive faces that did no good whatever. She finally got up and changed her place, dragging her notebook and bag three or four seats over, and struggling with a coat draped around her shoulders.

"Does my smoking bother you?" Carswell asked.

"Did Freud invent psychoanalysis? Did Roosevelt give us the New Deal?"

A Jewish intellectual had once given Swirling the key to comprehension of the Yiddishe mama idiom. It was that they never gave you a direct answer, but always couched their responses in large, roundabout ironies. Mrs. Lapidus tended to bear out such an analysis. "Did W. C. Fields drink?" she added as she settled herself again. Carswell laughed good-naturedly and tapped a clump of ash into his inkwell. Just then Dick Rubber walked in.

If he had a dog, and the dog bore out the legendary tendency of masters to choose pets for their similarity to themselves, then what awaited Rubber at home was surely a Saint Bernard. The resemblance was so striking that Swirling would not have been surprised to see him enter on all fours, with a brandy keg slung around his neck. It wasn't just the shaggy head and deep grave eyes. There was the same air of preoccupied solicitude we seem to find in the breed, as though they have a thousand things to do, not alone in the

Alps, more important than shambling about town on a leash, or sitting slavering in an automobile while their mistresses shop. Rubber struck the same note of hard-pressed dedication as he bustled in, breathing heavily from a climb up the stairs, slung his briefcase onto the teacher's desk, and settled his great bulk in the chair, having already begun the session by flinging out the question with which he had closed the previous.

"'Do I dare to eat a peach?' Well? Is it poetry? Bunch?"

A moment of collective guilt encompassed the class: few had given the matter much intervening thought. One of the twins spoke up.

"Well, it has to be poetry."

"Why so?"

"Because it doesn't sound like it, so it has to be picked from a specific poem because the question is obviously a trick one."

"Oh? What kind of poem?"

"About some pernickety pipsqueak beneficiary of a rotten society that engages in nothing but self-indulgence and can't get it up."

"Who can't get what up, this society or this pernickety beneficiary of yours?"

"Neither," the other sister chimed. "He's got nothing better to do than worry whether he'll dribble down his shirtfront while millions starve. Or just play with himself. He's been jerkin' the gherkin."

That brought a round of laughter, in which Rubber joined. He liked to see a class immediately ignited by something, a fire roaring in the grate the instant a match is touched to it.

"All very fine theoretically, but riddled with certain assumptions. What the General Semanticists call signal reactions. You respond very well, but from an established set of predilections. In the first place, why assume it's a man who's soliloquizing — though your sensing it is a soliloquy is quite

47

right — and secondly, how do we know the line wasn't written two hundred years ago, when there wasn't this third world you're worried about. Rightly, of course. Mrs. Lapidus?"

She had raised her hand, and now slid out from under her desk and stood in the aisle, apparently taking the Back to School literally by reciting like an elementary-grade pupil.

"This is ah digression before we get even started on the problem, wot's dis line," she said. "Not that there aren't two ways of lookink at de metter. So it's justified. Only today I am heving an argument wit ah fry cook who is servink me ah hamburger dot's burned to ah cinder. When I refuse to eat it *or* pay, he says, 'You ordered well done, ma'am.' I says, 'Not ah clinker. Put it in the esh can wit my compliments.' He got mad and says, 'You should be ashamed of yourself, treatink food like dis while millions starve,' and I says, 'Dot makes it all de more disgraceful what you do wit perfectly good food here. Dot's de crime.' So these thinks come op, and there are always two ways of lookink at it. So I agree with the younk ladies, but whether we can take the proletarian point of view with this line of poetry is another metter. I am also agreeing it's most likely ah trick question, so it has to be poetry just because it doesn't sound like it. Thenk you."

"Not necessarily," Rubber said as she sat down. "It might be something in prose though having the force of poetry in its context. Or it might be in a poem while not deserving the description 'poetic' at all. Classic poetry is full of flatter lines than that. Well, gang? Any more comments, guesses, surmises, speculations, what have you?" He always banked on the class's ignorance as necessary to the relish with which he anticipated filling the void with his instruction.

Here a hesitant glance of Becky's in Swirling's direction brought him Dick Rubber's attention as well.

"I see we have a guest auditing the course tonight. Mr. —"

"Swirling," Becky said. "He's a guest of mine."

"Glad to have you aboard, Mr. Swirling. What do you say? Do you think it's poetry?"

"Yes."

"Why?"

"Because it isn't anything else."

"Can you explain?"

Swirling found himself standing in the aisle too, taking Mrs. Lapidus's cue as indicative of normal custom here. Now he shone again with the pleasure of a schoolboy confident of reciting something he had fully boned up on.

"It's from T. S. Eliot's 'Love Song of J. Alfred Prufrock,' of course. A prime example of the *vers de société* of his early period," he began, causing Dick Rubber's eyes to narrow dangerously at the threat of an interloping wise ass undercutting an entire evening's lecture on the antipoetic in poetry which he had prepared himself for delivery to his cherished ignoramuses.

"'I have measured out my life with coffee spoons' would be another example of the exquisitely prosaic from the same poem," Swirling continued with galling fluency, "an example of how the moderns — we moderns — were housecleaning poetry of the fustian of traditional rhetoric, and of Eliot's own ideal of the 'objective correlative,' that of embodying an idea, or feeling, in a concrete image. Now then. Four, no, I'm sorry, five years later came *The Waste Land*, and between these two twentieth-century landmarks Eliot banished forever the idea that poetry required a special poetic diction. Oh, not that he hadn't predecessors. Frost, Pound and the Imagists, even Edwin Arlington Robinson in his way."

Swirling paused to grasp his lapels, as though needing some support to prevent his toppling over under the weight of all this erudition acquired in a mere half week's time. Everyone else had now swung aside to face him, reconstituting the classroom so as to make him the lecturer and Dick Rubber one of the scholars. He spotted a dark change in

Rubber's face, a distinct shift from the benignity first noted. He now reminded you of a dog that is both wagging its tail and barking at you. Swirling suddenly divined what had happened. He had put Rubber in the position of an after-dinner speaker who finds a predecessor spouting all his prepared stuff, some of it word for word, since he would have drawn from the same standard sources as those to which Swirling had flown. To go on would hardly be cricket, and might be dirty pool; yet to stop now was impossible, what with his hearers hanging on his every word — and transfixed at the moment on this pregnant pause. So he cleared his throat and forged ahead.

"Slicing it thin and laying it on the line soon became a principle whose violation meant old hat in the other arts as well, for poetry is our bellwether," he expounded. "Did not Eliot's deflationary use of famous lines from the major poets of antiquity anticipate what a decade later came to be known in jazz as swinging the classics? Well, sir, gone were the flamboyant gesture, the overstated case. Hemingway, Sherwood Anderson, others, were giving us understatement in the kindred realm of fiction, while . . ." The shore for which he tried to swim seemed to recede with every stroke. Still he groped for some point at which to stop and sit down, at the same time trying to keep a coherent grip on the thought sequence to which he had committed himself.

"Of course there are exceptions, but even the cakewalking grandiloquence of Wallace Stevens and Faulkner's verbal jags as well give us rhetoric with this new difference. Even rhetoric can be . . . be restrained, played down, somehow kept on ice, don't you know. In any case, no longer would novelists give us romantically plotted hokum, short story writers contrived endings," he resumed after a long breath, "or painters sentimentally confected landscapes. No longer would actors chew the scenery — they would throw their lines away. No longer would a thief say, 'Your money or your life!' He would be too self-conscious. The grand manner was out, all along the line. 'Stick 'em up!' must henceforth suffice. The conversational style was in." Rubber ground his teeth in wretched dismay: this was bang-up stuff. The reproach in his eyes was a dog's reproach. Yet Swirling swept remorselessly on, a doomed man doing his turn in what would no doubt be one of his last chances to shine. His own life was being measured out with coffee spoons, and precious little left in the canister! "And it is one of the more amusing ironies of the twentieth-century artistic revolution that while lingering Victorians were belting out clichés in exalted verbiage the moderns were baffling the man in the street with his own language. Everyone knows what Tennyson means when he raves about 'Summer isles of Eden lying in dark-purple spheres of sea.' But when Prufrock says 'Do I dare to eat a peach?,' heads are scratched and questions come to Mr. Eliot from the floor."

Here an ominous purple suffused Dick Rubber's face, as though he might be going to have an apoplectic fit and have to be carried out. Swirling hurried on, spotting a point at which he could round off what he had said.

"Because it so happens that a friend of mine, if I may interject a personal note here, attended a reading of Eliot's, his last in New York I believe." Swirling released one of his lapels long enough to pinch his nose and smile at the floor, in the manner of public raconteurs skilled at telegraphing to the audience that a slightly humorous note is about to be struck. "Well, sir, it was during the question period afterward that a woman got up and asked Eliot to explain that very line, the one we're considering tonight. Our Golden Text, as we used to call it in Sunday school."

"And what did Eliot say it meant?" Rubber asked in terror. He now feared nothing less than the total collapse of his prepared lecture. His face was like a bad eggplant.

"Ah, I'm sorry," Swirling said, glad not to have to pitch

Rubber an unexpected curve via the poet himself. "The friend in relating the incident, to my wife and me, couldn't for the life of her recall Eliot's exact reply. Except that his interpretation of the line differed from that to which the woman had always held. Which Eliot said was O.K. with him. Anything she thought — or we. Which puts us back where we started, and I for one am eager to hear some opinions tonight, especially Mr. Rubber's! Thank you."

He sat down to a round of applause heartily joined in by Rubber, if not led off by him, whether ironically or otherwise. Rubber seized the initiative as best he could by resolutely opening a book and proceeding to read the poem from beginning to end. When he came to the assigned line he gave it no more emphasis than required, letting it fall properly into place in the sequence.

"Well, there it is," he said when finished. "One of the perfect gems in the English language, those which plumb no depths and soar to no heights, but are consummate expressions of a given theme or reality — the reality in this case being the characterization itself. We need to know no more about Prufrock. My original question was not what the line *means*, but since we've got off on that foot, what *do* we think about Prufrock, in terms of what we know about him? Mrs. Tingle?"

"As a woman, we know what it'd be like to be on the receiving end of such a quote love song unquote," said Becky, who had raised her hand but didn't get up. "Because the title is obviously ironic. The lady in question will get nothing from old J. Alfred, there's no percentage in him, forget it. He's a dried prune, don't make him nervous with talk about romance. He's asexual, a-emotional, apolitical and a-everything else. Even just sinking his teeth into a peach for him would be positively Dionysian. A woman once said to Shaw, he was a vegetarian of course, 'Bernard, if you ate a lamb chop not a woman in the British Isles would be safe.'

We girls will be safe from Prufrock even if he eats that peach. It's obvious that Eliot is poking fun of this — this — dehydrated intellectual. Or is that too strong?"

"A little perhaps, but not too," Rubber said. "The fact is that the poem is a comedy, and anyone who has heard the recording of Eliot reading it knows that Eliot has his tongue as deep in his cheek as he can get it. You're right, Prufrock is effete. Uptight we'd say today. Inhibited. Probably puritanical. To one critic, the name suggests a condensation of 'prudent' and 'frock.' In his exegesis of the poem, Spender makes the point that the boundaries of Prufrock's world are strictly defined by what people think of him and what he might and ought to do, and so he has to think twice about even such a thing as eating a peach. But now what of our twin friends in this connection? Does the poet's satirization of his character satisfy them that justice has been done from the revolutionary point of view?"

"No, because look who's talking," the first twin said. "Eliot himself was a fascist, a Jew baiter —"

"Oh, come now."

"Well, anti-Semitic and a reactionary member of the Establishment. I've read that more than once. He wouldn't come out against Franco during the Spanish war."

"Why is it we always get to that word Establishment no matter what the discussion is?" Burt Winkleheart protested. "Incidentally, I wonder how many of us know that the word was first used by Emerson — who, incidentally, closed his eyes whenever he smiled — certainly a sign of maladjustment. Thank you."

There was some political rough-and-tumble which Rubber finally cut short, with a timely assist from Mrs. Lapidus, who rose again, this time to leave for her psychodrama group, which, due to a misfortune in scheduling, started when this session was half through. She reverted briefly to the point of Prufrock's being a failed romantic before leaving, or rather as

53

she slowly exited, like an actress skillfully stringing out a valedictory speech.

"If itting piches is ah symbol romentic impulses, dot's provink male zest, I guess I'm ah lucky woman. Last night my husband climbed out of bed saying he was starved, went to the kitchen, and ate ah hull can freestones. Ah. Hull. Can. So my adwice to the lady he's soliloquizing to is, get out now from dot schlep. Anybody who's afraid somebody is going to drop ah question on his plate, he's not going to pop one! Thenk you. Good night, all."

The group broke up a half hour later, when Rubber had his composition workshop. Swirling stopped on his way out to thank him for an interesting and instructive evening, and to apologize for his loquacity. Facing about, Rubber laid first one paw then both on Swirling's shoulders, and breathing an air of mint-flavored forgiveness said, "That's all right. Saved me a lot of gab. You added a lot to the session. Come again."

As Swirling and Becky made their way down the corridor to the front entrance, his eye was caught by a sign on a closed classroom door which read: "No admittance. Problem in progress." A voice coming from inside sounded familiar. They paused to listen. It was Mrs. Lapidus, taking her turn as psychodrama subject for the evening. "Ah. Hull. Can," she was saying.

They went out of the building into a cold and starry night.

"It wasn't a problem to her in our class," Becky said. "How will they act it out in there? But what I kept wondering was whether Lapidus ate them straight out of the can or what. Do you have your car?"

"No, I walked. Only a few blocks."

"It's pretty chilly. I have my VW."

"I was hoping to stretch my legs."

As they made their way toward where the car was parked, the backs of their hands accidentally touched, and after a

54

moment Swirling turned his palm around to take hers. She gave a responsive squeeze, and then with a laugh hiked his arm up and tucked it under hers. "It's still early. And such a glorious night. Look at all those diamonds up there."

"Can we go to your place?"

"Are you completely?"

"What do you mean?"

"My brother's visiting me. I thought you knew." Her answer quickened his hopes rather than dashed them, because of her instant interpretation of his suggestion.

"Let's take a ride to the beach," he said.

"O.K. Pick up a carton of coffee and some doughnuts from that diner on the way. They're homemade."

They sat with their coffee and doughnuts in a parking spot at the beach where they were fairly secluded, listening to the plash of the waves and watching a crescent moon rise. They chatted nervously about the evening's seminar, Swirling's hoarse voice especially betraying the emotion clotting his throat. He climbed out to empty their debris into a nearby trash can that was ringed with beer bottles and other assorted litter, as though we were a nation of near-missers, conscientious enough only to heave our waste in the general direction of the container, or to slow our automobiles only long enough to chuck it out the window as we go by. Thinking of Enid's environmentally dedicated evening caused him a twinge, and he stooped to pitch a few empty bottles into the barrel. A penitential gesture for sins not yet committed. A cold wind stung his cheeks and whipped his hair, and drove a grain of sand into one eye, which he managed to blink away. He flapped his arms humorously inside his fleece-lined storm coat, though he removed that before climbing back into the car. Simple embraces in a VW would be cumbersome enough while Becky still bulked large in her own pony-hide coat, and she wriggled out of that as he sat down. They threw both garments into the back seat. In all the jostle a breath of her perfume filled the air, a scent so gently pervasive that he asked what it was. "Femme," she said, pronouncing the word as though it were "fem." She also said "crape suzette." Oh, well, his own French was no bargain either.

She swung around to face him, drawing her knees up onto the seat.

"I guess this doesn't have anything to do with the price of eggs, does it? I mean I'm not married, so for me — I mean it's no great moral sweat. But, um."

She could have been called a small birdlike woman, but he noticed how perfectly shaped was the nose which would chiefly have given rise to the description, how finely set between the narrow but fully curving mouth and the round gray eyes. They watched him with the clear implication that the ball was in his court. Then she smiled the mischievous girl smile, with the closed lips bunched to one side. He reached out and laid a hand on her shoulder, as though he were going to administer a chastening word or take an apologetic turn of thought for the circumstances in which they found themselves. Instead he teased the rim of her blouse delicately downward with his thumb, until he could feel her cool white skin. He removed his hand, only to lower it and press softly what it grazed on. There was nothing under the blouse. He could sense the perfection of her little breasts through its silk. They were like quicksilver under his palm. He drew his hand away again, kissing her, this time to work her blouse up from under the slacks into which it was tucked. "Oh, my God," he whispered, fondling the twin treasures at last. "A pair of baby doves."

She whispered in his ear, "You're making Becky Tingle."

He pretended he hadn't heard, even though it made his flesh creep. He must not be so fastidious, noting discrediting signs and counteraphrodisiac details, letting everything give him the willies. He was no Prufrock, nor was meant to be.

Not for him the premonitory qualm, the exquisite hesitation. He ate Becky's peaches while foraging for even more paradisal fruit, clawing with relative success at zippers and buttons and snaps until, there against his foraging palm, were the sweet flaring hindquarters, the flawlessly sculptured arc of the thigh, the fragrant fringed cleft, the moist pink flower within. She twisted about to flatten as much of her front against his as she could, when he gave notice of wanting to graze a moment on that dream of a derrière. She tightened like a bowstring, and he could feel his own every muscle and sinew harden in their common tension. Hotly into his mouth she panted something about seizing the moment — then something about — No Tomorrow.

That was it, he thought. *She knows, and this instant riotous unqualified surrender is the gift not of one but of two women locked in unsuspected collaboration, and I with each alone and both together in my winter's boon, freely given and gratefully taken*, he thought, and then thought no more about it as they rushed together into that First Garden to which kind nature lets us intermittently return, the primordial Eden to whose gates Sin — so far from being the cause of our exile — is often as not the very key. What rubbish! And how deliriously true!

Had Becky been any less dainty, much more would scarcely have been possible in a Volkswagen, even with her lying diagonally back, half wedged under the steering wheel, and the stick shift set in reverse position, at the upper left, in order to give Swirling a few more inches in which to maneuver. There is always an element of distraction about a first sexual encounter, even without distractions, such as banging his crazy bone on the steering wheel in the midst of one manipulation, and a sharp pain dealt across the base of his spine by the underside of the dashboard, as he tried to work his way around to a more advantageous position. There was also, with Swirling, as with many men, the problem of being

57

mentally distracted in the very act of love — that is, by irrelevant associations of the most grotesque kind coming at the most inappropriate moments. As he struggled and strove to mount his now passionate mate, he remembered a scene of some congestion on a train he was riding through Italy a number of years before. A large Italian family were eating lunch from a variety of paper bags presided over by a portly father, and at the end of the meal the father rolled a salami sausage up in his cap before stowing it away in one of the sacks. He had recalled the scene many times, but never under circumstances as incongruous as this.

"Oh, Bobolink!"

"What?"

Again he refused to believe the testimony of his senses, much less the larger chilling implication that this was to be her pet name for him. She was given to the diminutive in addressing friends (no doubt because she was that herself), so that every Tom, Dick and Harry became Tommy, Dicky and — well, you couldn't do anything much with Harry. But they had a mutual friend named Peter, whom most called Pete, but she called Peterkin. Swirling had frequently been Bobby, which was enough. Now there was more — borderline unendurable. He was to be her Bobolink, and every time he heard it he died a little, every time he heard it he paid — another installment of interest on his moral debt.

Was it worth it? To that he would have replied in Mrs. Lapidus's method of counterinterrogation. "Did he go back for more?" Not for him the reductive aphorism of the Englishman (Lord Palmerston?) who said life would be tolerable if it were not for its pleasures. That was already Prufrock country. No, he would string along with the mythic view of sex, safe in the custody of the man in the street: "Even when it's no good it's good."

Becky said: "I always had you figured for a puritan."

"It's never too late to mend your ways."

She lay back against the door, in roughly the position in which she'd been possessed, one foot still mired in a leg of her slacks, having in her haste peeled down only the other. She looked decidedly wanton. It was the only time he himself had ever made love with all his clothes on, and as she sat up now and wriggled back into hers, it struck him that they must resemble the high-school students in the other cars parked at intervals along the town's lovers' lane. Back to school indeed!

"Shall I take you home?"

"Maybe just as far back as the school. I can use the walk."

"I see what you mean."

After being dropped off, he ran the few blocks to his house. He was relieved to see it dark, Enid not yet back. He hurried up the front steps, the door key ready in his hand, then galloped through the house turning lights on. He was sitting in the living room in his pajamas, reading, when she arrived. He was pacing in his Groucho stalk, flourishing a cigar, when she came in the door.

"Well! Do you realize what time it is? I suppose you ran into your old WAC sergeant and sat around in some bar till you lost all track of it. A fine how-do-you-do this is, and one more like it and it'll be goodbye. And look at the way you're dressed. That dress is becoming, but when will the rest of it be coming? And look at those stockings with that pair of slippers. Don't you know that with those pumps you need the right hose? Do you realize this is the third time this month you've come home at this hour? Do you want to kill me? Do you want to kill your mother? Come to think of it that might not be a bad idea. I see all your family except you. Take your brother — anywhere! Why do people get married anyway? Because they want each other the worst way, and believe me that's it. . ."

"It's coming along O.K.," Enid said, smiling as she shook her coat off. "Especially the voice — and the diction too.

That 'third' and 'worst' almost, but not quite, 'thoid' and 'woist.' In between in a way you couldn't spell phonetically. Like the New York 'irl' for 'oil.' Of course with the greasepaint mustache and eyebrows the illusion will be better. I suppose you'll part your hair straight out to the sides from the middle. But you realize that benefit is only a month off? How much stuff have you got?" Hanging her coat up in the closet she asked, "How was the class?"

"Educational. Tell you about it later. How was the meeting?"

"Long. Since I agreed with most of the other soapbox orators I saw no need to speak my piece. I'm sure we'll block the factory, though they had some pious poop of a vice-president there giving their solemn word they'll make sure nothing gets polluted."

"Speaking of getting polluted," he resumed, flicking the cigar, "it's a long time since you and I tied one on together. What do you say we get quietly sozzled some night soon? Oh, incidentally, that aunt of mine in Toledo died and left me eleven million dollars. Now I can buy you that yacht, or a nice hanky or something. It just goes to show you — where there's a will there's a way. Now let's turn out the lights and go to bed, but don't expect too much. I gave at the office."

Four

THAT HE CONTINUED to see Becky Tingle was viewed as mitigating rather than compounding his offense. A sustained entanglement was certainly more to one's credit — or at least less to one's discredit — than a casual fling, casually forgotten.

The problem of rendezvous eased when Becky's brother Pomfret left, at any rate for a while. Swirling generally worked at home, but he could explain any absence from it as necessitated by his having to run in to the city to the office of the sports magazine for which he mainly wrote, or the need to visit the library there for research, or to interview somebody. Then he would pedal toward the railroad station on his bicycle, but halfway there veer off in the direction of Becky's place, by long force of habit turning his head to catch the aphorism on the bulletin board of the Presbyterian church as he sped by. "If a care isn't big enough to turn into a prayer, it's too small to be made into a burden," it had stood for some time now, showing a falling off of inspiration as well as evidence of running to fat. The inspirationals had normally been far pithier as well as more frequently changed.

At Becky's he generally hid the bike behind a row of willows overhanging a fence in the back yard — actually her front yard. Because she rented a garage apartment, and to avoid the prying eye of the landlady, Mrs. Pesky, he would bend over double as he shot by the bay window at the side of the main house, like a cyclist in a six-day race. The bike concealed, he remained screened among the willow boughs himself a moment, to make sure no faces were watching from the main house. The fact that the windows there had lace curtains for some reason made any inhabitants lurking behind them seem more morally critical, and more to be feared by wrongdoers, than if they had been peering out between contemporary draperies. Too, there was a back porch, and people with porches were inclined to hold more rigid views than those with terraces and patios. One could more easily slip uncensored past onlookers suspended in butterfly chairs nibbling canapés than by Mrs. Pesky, a gauntlet of one who — final clue to formidability — hung her wash out on the line. The angle of the garage apartment in relation to the house also posed a problem in remaining foot transit, the problem of keeping his face from being seen and possibly recognized in the brief sprint across the no-man's-land to Becky's place. Swirling always ran up the flight of stairs to her landing sideways, in fact almost backwards, like a figure in a movie film run in reverse. But at last there would be Becky waiting to greet him at the door in a flowered kimono, or half a pair of pajamas, or nothing at all.

Then it was like going to bed with a lighted firecracker. A string of firecrackers. Her climactic cries were such that Swirling often feared they might fetch Mrs. Pesky in person, or that she would have the police pelting up the stairs on suspicion of a malefactor in the apartment committing bodily violence. So he always made sure the windows were closed, and then sometimes had to put a hand over her mouth. Her crises were so frequent as to seem almost continuous, and her lovemaking as such was accompanied by a steady rhapsodic gush, actually a sort of graduation of her normal speech. She liked some counterpart of this from her partner as well, being one of those women who must have the sexual experience verbalized — not later, talking about "how it was" while foraging for food, etc., but en route. "What are we doing now? What are you doing to me now? Oh, what next?" she would pant in wild inquiry as she thrashed in his embrace like a bronco trying to throw its rider. Swirling had soon pasted together an all-purpose repertory of lyric material on which to draw: fragments of erotic poetry, vivid descriptive touches or scraps of heated dialogue from bed scenes in novels he had read, some gamy street stuff and drugstore cowboy waggeries ("Spread your legs a little, honey, you're pinching my ears."), all intermingled with original material of his own, often forged impromptu in the heat of the moment. And it all went into a reserve hopper for later use, since not to repeat oneself was impossible. He was plowing her this, he was churning her that. He would rave about that slashed plum, that halved strawberry, that succulent bivalve about to swallow him whole, about pollinating that flower whose nectar he had sipped. He divided her into temperate, semitropic and tropical zones, with salutes to her steaming equatorial thicket and the hot blossom nestled within. The required metaphors tumbled out of him every which way, mixed and unmixed. He felt like both a puffing athlete and a commentator giving a blow-by-blow account of his performance, and then he became still a third self, observing himself doing all this, the spectator for whom the game is played and the color broadcast. What was her backside? A moonflower. Her mouth? A chord of crimson music (Cummings?). What was her breast? A caught bird fluttering in his palm. The other? Same thing. What was he plunging into now? Her gloxinia, trumpet vine, rose of Sharon, wet with her own dew now about to take his own. "Oh, Bobolink!" When she uttered that pet name for him, his own paroxysms were a matter of half squirming with embarrassment. She made his flesh creep even as she sent him into orbit.

One day, when their first storm of passion was spent, there were footsteps drumming on the wooden stairs outside and then a knock on the door as someone gained the landing.

"Sheesh."

"You're not going to answer it, are you?" he said.

She rose and stole toward a bedroom window offering a view of the landing, where, peering out from behind a drawn shade, she announced, "It's Mrs. Pesky, looking more oblong than ever." Presently there was another knock, and then finally footsteps descending. Becky bent over the bed and playfully snicked his depleted stem with her finger. "Like a tassel. Cute. It'll be good as new in an hour though. Till then, good buddy, I, let's see what there is to, do you like tuna fish sandwiches?"

Lying on his side like a beached fish, his mouth mashed against the pillow, he could see a magazine on a chair, open to a fashion plate showing a spruce executive having his shoes shined in his office, while glancing at his wristwatch with a sense of implied appointments. Swirling was anxious to get away. Not eager to, as 63 percent of the American Heritage Dictionary Usage Panel insisted, but anxious to: *Angst* was more than 63 percent of his postlove *tristesse*. He must shop for a watch to give his father as a birthday present. He would take it Sunday to the retirement home where his father stayed. A last visit? He remained prey to bathetic associations, some even worse than the Italian paterfamilias on the train wrapping the salami in his cap. He remembered his half-blind old grandmother when she was staying with them in their house in old Kazoo, pouring milk over some dry dog food, under the impression that it was breakfast cereal. He had set the poor dear straight, a boy of ten or twelve tenderly wresting the dish from her grasp and fixing her a bowl of Grape Nuts to eat. The next day he found her pouring Grape Nuts into the dog's dish.

He sat propped up on two pillows, a position commanding a view through the open bedroom doorway into part of the kitchen. Becky was standing over the table fixing their sandwiches. In the middle distance, beyond the doorway but neatly framed in it, she resembled a figure in a Dutch domestic genre painting, the composition completed and perfected by the refrigerator half incorporated in it. They were playing house. They were ten or eleven. She was the girl on his block, and she had just drawn from the icebox a large blue crock covered with what looked like a shower cap. With a knife or spatula she was scooping tuna fish salad out of it and onto slices of appetizing-looking dark bread, spreading it out to the crusts neatly, like a bricklayer with his trowel and mortar. Light rimmed the curve of her naked flank, the compact bubble of her belly, and the tilted breasts. There had been some talk of coating them with honey for his delectation, but nothing had come of it. Perhaps next time. Feet could be heard toiling up the wooden stairs again, and, after a pause during which a head cocked listening could be well imagined, another knock.

"Sheesh."

Licking her fingers Becky came back to the bedroom for her kimono, signaling for him to relax and stay where he was, not pop under the bed or into a closet like a character in a French farce. Swirling groaned faintly.

"— wondering if you were all right," Mrs. Pesky could be heard inquiring at the open door. "Because I saw a rather odd —" Something unintelligible here, and then, "sneaking around, like."

"No, it's O.K. I have a friend visiting me. Was it a man?"

"Sort of."

"Then that's him."

"The way he snuck —"

"That's him. Thanks just the same."

"Because there have been so many robberies. I just wanted to make sure you were home."

"I'm home — as you can see. And my car. Thanks a lot, Mrs. Pesky."

He was sitting on the edge of the bed when Becky walked in with two sandwiches on a plate. She let her robe fall away as she nuzzled his face with her breasts. "What are they?"

"Blancmanges."

"That's what you said before."

"I know. I didn't want to be caught in any discrepancies."

"Try again. The girl likes, um, variation."

"Then they are croquettes."

"Swell."

"Absolutely perfectly pyramidal little croquettes, to be devoured, but never consumed. Eaten up, but always there."

He gobbled one dutifully, to show her what he meant.

"These are stimulating conversations we have."

"And how."

"Now you can have your sandwich."

There was another rap on the door.

"Sheesh."

She handed Swirling the plate and went to the door.

"I see a bicycle down there, hidden behind the willow trees. Do you know anything about that?"

"It belongs to my gentleman caller. He always hides it

because, like you say, they steal everything these days. He doesn't want anybody to see it, put temptation in their way?"

"The neighborhood is going to pot. He ought to hide it better. Maybe put it in the garage. Because I could see it."

"I'll tell him. Thanks again . . . Sheesh."

Under the circumstances, Swirling couldn't very well turn up at home before seven o'clock or so. Arriving about then would mean he had taken the six-ten. It was now just short of five. They curled up under the covers and took a nap. He dreamed that he and Becky were together changing the epigram on the bulletin board of the Presbyterian church. The lettering became gibberish. He awoke feeling her rekindling in his arms. She ran a hand along his back, up his thighs, coaxing him back to life. He was about to prise her legs apart with his knee and ease himself inside her when there was again a knock on the door.

"Oh, sheesh."

"Don't answer it."

"It's best to."

She again padded out in her kimono, snapping on a light or two as she made her way to the door, for dusk had fallen. It was here that Swirling began to experience her really devilish knack for intrigue.

"It's not there now — the bicycle," Mrs. Pesky reported. "I thought you ought to know. I just happened to look as I went to throw out the trash. It's gone."

"So is my friend."

A blank silence — as of someone silenced — and then Mrs. Pesky said, "Oh, I see. Then he . . . I was afraid somebody took it, and that I ought to tell you."

Swirling could sense the duplicity in Mrs. Pesky's voice, and though he had never laid eyes on her close up — only enough to confirm that she was most oblong — he could visualize her expression of chagrin. Becky had her dead to rights, as much as telling her, with a sly glance Swirling could more clearly conjure, that she knew the woman had been nosily keeping an eye on goings-on in the guesthouse. By the same token, Mrs. Pesky had the unseen Swirling dead to rights. She knew he hadn't left or she wouldn't have reported the theft. She therefore also knew Becky was lying. So the score stood Mrs. Pesky 2; Home Team, 1 — a little better than a standoff from her point of view.

"Probably one of the neighborhood kids," Becky told him when she returned. "Do you want to report it?"

"What, to the police? Hell no. I'd have to say where it was taken. I'll just say when I got back to the station it was missing."

"Don't you bikers chain them to that rack there?"

"Mine was filed off with a hacksaw, or the lock was shot. Oh, Christ." He sighed, nervously casting a glance at a clock on the dresser. There were so many angles to think of, so much story to concoct, taking care to avoid any slipup or fallacy that might catch him out or get him in the soup. Something like panic began to take hold of him, and the need to be out of here was not far from the wish that he hadn't come at all. The feeling of entrapment focused on Becky in a subtly shifted imputation of blame that he quite recognized. This was paradise certified. The woman thou gavest me, he was close to saying, she made me eat the fruit of the forbidden tree. And the fruit momentarily eaten, the temptress was no longer that, rather something to be fled as quickly as possible. But why these feelings of guilt if all this had Enid's tacit approval?

"I'll take you to the station," she said, collecting the plate and some glasses. She carried them calmly to the kitchen. "You got off the train and found your bicycle had been stolen. What time did you get in?" she asked, grooming him in rehearsal.

"Pretty soon," Swirling said, suddenly deciding that he

had taken the four-forty and would be pulling in any minute. He began to dress. "We'd better leave."

Dusk had deepened into an early winter nightfall as he descended the stairs beside Becky, keeping her between him and the golden glow of Mrs. Pesky's cozy kitchen window. Becky laughed when he turned his coat collar up and his hat brim down. "You look like a ham in a spy picture," she said. "I suppose," he said, and darted around to a spot beside the garage where her car was parked, also under the draping willow trees. She smiled to herself as they bounced along toward the road, Swirling by force of habit averting his face as they passed the bay window. She looked more than ever like a mischievous child outwitting the grown-ups. How had he ever got mixed up with her? When could he see her again?

A crowd pacing the station platform and milling around a jam of parked cars indicated something was wrong. A man in a ski parka was gesticulating to a woman holding a leash on which a tiny dog twitched like a trout on the end of a line. Impatient drivers honked to be let through. Swirling had been a bit player in such mob scenes before, waiting for somebody overdue from town, sometimes with several trains backed up in a mass delay God knew where.

"I'll see what's what," he said. He hesitated with his hand on the door handle. "You can go. Becky, it's been —"

"Don't be sill. I'll wait till you find out what's what. People seem to be listening to radios. They have those commuter flashes. Mine's busted. Go see. Oh, for God's sake, you act like you've committed a — go *see*. Or do you want to wait here in hiding while I do?"

He walked over to a knot of people huddled around a station wagon with its radio going just as the news coming over it was also blared from loudspeakers on the station platform. He shuffled back with his bleak intelligence, steeled for another "Sheesh."

"There's been a fire in Grand Central tunnel and all the power's been shut off indefinitely. There are no trains leaving till further notice."

"Hm." His own brain refusing to function, or spinning vainly like wheels in a snow rut, he sat watching Becky tap her fingers on the steering wheel, the bee-stung mouth screwed to one side in thought. People, mostly women come for husbands, began to get back into their cars and drive off. The speed with which a plan of action was formulated in Becky's head displayed again her talent for conspiracy.

"Find out what the last train is that got out. O.K.? Probably the three-ten. You obviously didn't take that back. So, um — you can't go home again."

"*What?*"

"Husbands stranded in town stay in hotels. Or get soused in the Biltmore bar till eleven or twelve or when the trains start up again. So we'll have to go back to my place and keep in touch on the radio. Or you can keep phoning for the dope. Keep on top of the situation that way. But, um. I mean it's no sweat. You just find out which you're going to do — sit in the Biltmore bar waiting for action, or take a room there."

He turned to look at her in blank amazement.

"Then what?"

"Oh, sheesh. You call home saying which it is, a or b. If it's b, then we can spend the night together. Won't that be nice? Bobolink?"

It was the latter. He was stuck in town. Becky fried a chicken and baked a few potatoes, and they drank two bottles of white Burgundy. By then it was ten o'clock.

"Now you can have your blancmange," she said, getting up from the table.

Back in her double bed, she stroked his cheek and ruffled his hair, as though undecided whether he should be lulled or stimulated. At last she took his hand in hers and began to draw it gently across her body, stroking herself with it, using it as though it were a garden tool. Finally she settled it on her intended target.

"What are you doing now?"

"Falling asleep," he said, trying to mumble the words drowsily though in fact he lay stark awake, wondering what would happen if Enid took a notion to telephone him at the Biltmore, and listening to the wind in Mrs. Pesky's willows going *sheesh, sheesh . . .*

Five

AMONG THE THINGS that popped inopportunely into mind when he was making love — a snapshot once seen of Proust humorously strumming a tennis racket as though it were a banjo, a production of Wagner he had attended in which the Rhine Maidens sang on a hydroelectric power dam — of all these, the worst by far was an incident so awful he thought seriously of consulting a hypnotist who claimed successes in expunging from conscious memory the recollection of embarrassments too oppressive for his clients to bear.

He had just showered, on a hot summer day, and was traipsing naked around the house, trailing a towel and whistling along with a jazz band going on the radio, when the doorbell rang. He had locked the door in fear of being walked in on by a friend — one of the klatschers given not only to dropping in, but to walking in with only a knock and a called-out "Hello." It was an old-world custom his grandparents had imported from Holland. They would open the door and call, "Volk? Volk tehuis?" Any folk at home? A quick glance out the window having revealed a station wagon the spit of their own, Swirling naturally thought it was Enid back from her shopping. It was in the early days of their marriage, when he was still full of a randy bridegroom's incidental japes and didoes. Tomfooleries such as his saying to the bride on their wedding night, "This is indeed a pleasure." Now, chuckling to himself as he went to the door, he imagined the look on Enid's face when, framed between two sacks of groceries, she would get a load of him doing his comic strip — a burlesque of burlesque. The radio supplied a perfect beat for the round of bumps and grinds with which he made to greet her in the vestibule after flinging the door open. He swiveled his hips slowly around in a lascivious rhythm, the towel draping him, knotted at one corner. Then he snapped the towel free, dropped it to the floor, and thrust out his pelvis in one last, excruciating *bump*, his eyes closed in a trance and his hands laced behind his head.

"Hello. I'm Mrs. Balsam? From up the road? We're circulating this partition? To make the corner a four-way stop?"

He made a codpiece of his two hands, removing one long enough to slam the door shut as he backed away in horror. "Not today," he'd said, or some such, before getting down to the serious business of pacing the house while hammering the sides of his head with both fists. Should he kill himself? Murder old lady Balsam before she got much farther down the road with her damned partition? Move to another town? He never told Enid about the episode, and it acquired a little perspective soon afterward when Mrs. Balsam's husband died and she moved away herself, not before innumerable imagined conversations had branded themselves on his brain. ". . . never know about people. Someone you think is perfectly . . . pillar of . . . then one day . . . More tea? One o' them preeverts he was, I expect. One of them, you know, exhibitors they call them? I thought better of reporting it to the police. For her sake, you know, poor thing. Lord alone knows what sorts of things she has to, you know, *do*? I mind the time we lived in Nebraska, there was this character . . . nanny goat . . ."

Swirling was about to be dealt an embarrassment a hundred times worse even than that.

When Becky's brother Pomfret returned from whatever wanderings had been occupying him, the problem of rendezvous was revived. Then Becky announced she had the ideal trysting place. It was the empty house on Benson Road that she had extolled to Enid as an investment, the day Swirling had sensed his end to be near. The heir living in France had given the agency with which she was connected a few months' exclusive on it. It alone, she assured Bobolink, could show the property to prospective buyers for that period, after which, if not sold, it would be thrown on the open market for listing by all members of the local real estate board. So there would be no risk in their using it for an assignation for the time being, especially since her boss, the only other who could show it, was away at the moment, shelling on Sanibel Island.

"I've got the key," she told him one afternoon when he phoned. "Is now O.K. with you?"

"Fine." He seemed to be inaugurating affairs rather than putting them in order, but who would begrudge a man bound for his long home?

He had called from the railroad station, to which he had pedaled on his new bike, again officially headed for New York. He chained it to the parking rack and was waiting for her there when she swept up in the VW, the cherry mouth twisted in its asymmetrical little grin.

The house stood behind a high privet grievously in need of

barbering, and at the head of a serpentine flagstone walk in the crevices of which assorted herbs had been planted by a previous owner. "That's rosemary, that's, um, life everlasting," Becky said, identifying them as they wended their way to the door. "Basil."

She took him on a tour of the house, just as though he were a client, before they settled down on the floor of the truly soaring studio living room, on some blankets she had brought. They spread them near the cold hearth, as though before a roaring fire. She had also packed a small picnic hamper, and they nibbled on deviled eggs and nipped from a bottle of Chablis as they undressed, shivering playfully. The thermostat was kept at fifty-five, and they thought it best not to turn the furnace up. At last they stretched out between the blankets and began to make love.

"What are you doing now? What's he doing to our Becky?"

"Nibbling on your Nesselrodes."

"Now what are you doing?"

"Seeing who's outside," Swirling said, getting up and making his way to the window.

He fancied he had heard a car pull into the driveway, and sure enough, there was a lime-green sedan parked next to the shaggy privet. Two women were climbing out of it.

"I thought you said you had an exclusive on this place," he said, shielding his eyes against a slash of sunlight as he peered out. "That looks like Mrs. Tarbell with a client." Becky tripped over and joined him at the window. "Oh, my God, it's Enid!" he said. "She's going to show Enid the house! Oh, my God!"

His tongue was like a strip of rotted cloth he could hardly manipulate into articulate speech.

"Oh, sheesh," Becky gasped. "Oh, my God. They must have thrown it on the open market without my — Why wasn't I . . . ?"

Mrs. Tarbell, a tall bony woman in her sixties, was pointing out the merits of the house from outside, gesturing broadly and smiling as the two wound slowly up the walk.

"What'll we do?" Becky said, clutching her head in both hands.

Swirling was by now in his shorts and getting into his shirt, in the collar of which he had left his necktie when disrobing. It became entangled in his fingers as he frantically buttoned up, all knuckles. "Didn't she see the other car, figure there's another cluh — cluh — client inside? Wait till they've gone?" he squeaked, his teeth chattering with more than cold.

"Probably not. Maybe I shouldn't have left it on the road. They're coming in."

Swirling snatched up the rest of his clothes and shot through an intervening dining room to the kitchen, hoping there might be a key in the door there or that none was necessary from the inside, thus offering the possibility of escape out the back yard and over a fence. But there was no key, in a door that required one from both sides. He flipped the latch locking a window over the sink and tried to raise it, but it was stuck tight from a recent painting. Becky had picked up her own clothes by now and stood half naked in the doorway, watching him give a last vain heave at the unyielding sash. Voices outside reached the front door. She spun around and ran up the stairs to the second floor. Swirling had set his clothes on the sink in order to tussle with the window. He gathered them up again and made a beeline up the stairs after Becky, flashing out of sight just as the door opened and Mrs. Tarbell was heard to say, "I want to look at your face when you see the studio living room."

Instinct took them to the master bedroom, in Swirling's case because he remembered from the tour that its windows gave on the back yard, and as he wriggled into the rest of his clothes with the speed of a fireman he speculated on the possibility of shinnying down a drainpipe or even jumping to the ground, provided there was a clump of bushes or something to break his fall there. But they turned out to be casement windows which cranked open vertically, not quite enough for him to squeeze through. Besides, they were screened, not that that would have been a serious obstacle. He would have sailed through screens like a circus dog through paper hoops.

Fully dressed now, he stole on tiptoe down the hall to the other two bedrooms, to find the windows the same there, and even smaller. They were trapped. They were like doomed troops progressively more cornered by mop-up snipers in a beleaguered building. Voices drifted up steadily from below, where footsteps marked the passage of the other two from the living room (which elicited all the exclamations of delight that had been anticipated) to the kitchen.

"— can't for the life of me imagine who's been —" Mrs. Tarbell was saying. She was talking in a puzzled tone of the blankets and picnic hamper, which by now had been noticed. "Young people sometimes do break into these empty houses. They found a whole sort of commune in that old Caldwell mansion last year. Living up in the attic there, remember?"

"Yes, I remember that," Enid said. "Harmless though. Just a little self-service."

"Nothing seems to be broken into here." The knob of the kitchen door was tried with a rattle. "Very odd. None of the windows or doors jimmied. Most peculiar."

"It's a wonderful little house. Charming — to use that overworked word. How's the basement — dry?"

Swirling, who had rejoined Becky in the master bedroom, clasped his hands in a pantomime of ardent prayer, rolling his eyes to heaven. She nodded, catching his meaning. If Mrs. Tarbell was to show the cellar first, they had a chance.

They could steal downstairs, whip out the front door, and be off and away like a shot, undetected. But Mrs. Tarbell's voice was heard, dashing that hope.

"Let's go upstairs first." She stood below in the entrance-way and called up, "Is there anybody there? Yoo-hoo, anybody upstairs?"

They stood frozen in the middle of the bedroom, now hoping that apprehension might keep her from chancing the second story after the mysterious signs of vagabond occupancy. It didn't, and presently she was heard leading the way up. Swirling pointed to the closet, shoving Becky toward it with the other hand. It was a big one, running nearly the width of one end of the room, with two sliding doors. One stood open, and they hurried through that, Swirling drawing it shut after they were inside. They stood there in the dark, quiet as mice, hardly daring to breathe. There was one last slim chance: if it occurred to nobody to open the closet, they were home and dry. They might even be home and dry if only one door were slid open and they were crouching in the gloom behind the other.

With the real estate broker's natural sense of climax, Mrs. Tarbell was saving the master bedroom until last.

"I think casement windows are so charming," she could be heard remarking in the room across the hall. "Always remind me of that line of poetry, about magic casements opening on something or other. I forget the poet. Is it Shelley?"

"No, Keats," Enid said. "'Ode to a Nightingale.' 'Magic casements, opening on the foam of perilous seas, in faery lands forlorn,' I think. Yes, they are handsome windows. And I've always liked leaded panes."

The two now crossed the passage and strolled into the master bedroom. Its size was noted, also the larger windows, and the beautiful fireplace, Delft-tiled like the one downstairs.

"It's certainly nice," Enid said. "How much do you think a house like this could be rented for? Things keep going up so fast."

"Six hundred a month at *least*, and maybe more. I see the crank on this particular window is broken, but that's a small matter to fix."

That was the moment Enid chose to slide the closet door open. She nearly jumped out of her skin at the sight of Swirling standing there, mugging despairingly and bent a little at the knees to keep his head from hitting the crosspole. She gave a low involuntary gasp. Becky, also partly squatting, buried her face in her hands. Hideous as the moment was, it was still short of the absolute catastrophe it might have become had Mrs. Tarbell walked over to the closet and entered the drama. As it was, Enid recovered herself quickly enough to grasp instantly what Swirling meant with the dumb show he now made. He put a finger to his lips with a shushing face, while pointing frantically toward Mrs. Tarbell, fortunately still fiddling with the ailing window crank, her back to the scene. Enid calmly slid the door shut again, with a suitable comment about the capacity of the closet, and then after a last word regarding the bedroom itself, walked quickly out of it, followed by Mrs. Tarbell. She could be heard discoursing on the airy grace of the staircase as they slowly descended it.

All might still have been well, or at least not totally irreparable, had Swirling not tried to justify himself. Enid admitted to an extramarital brush or two of her own, simply deploring his deception about this one. That was a breach of faith in what they had vowed would be a completely open marriage.

"I understand that, being civilized and completely honest and aboveboard with each other and all," he said when they thrashed the whole thing out that evening. "It's just that I think, thought it best not to have the other person know, even though she tried to telegraph that she'd connive at a —"

"Other person, what other person?"

"You."

"Ah ha."

Enid always preferred to argue on her feet if at all feasible, and she looked almost unconscionably elegant as she leaned against the wall in persimmon-colored slacks and another of her black scoop-necked blouses, an elbow in the hollow of one hand as in the other she held a pencil-thin cigar, making the idea that she could ever be "wronged" preposterous. Swirling sat crumpled in his favorite armchair, trying to make out a case for himself. He debated whether now to pull out what was to be regarded as the principal stop in his defense. Enid hunched her shoulders, shifting the elbow in the palm that cupped it, and said, "I suppose she's a hot little piece?"

He nodded confirmation, closing his weary eyes. "She's a great lay, but she needs an editor."

Stiffening upward out of his slump, as though someone had prodded the underside of his chair with a poker, he drew out the principal stop.

"After all, it's not as though it were just another sheep-through-the-gap husband straying off into an affair. It's" — he came out with it — "call it the last fling of a dying man."

It caught Enid with a mouthful of smoke, which she held a moment as she rolled her great brown eyes away in an expression of puzzled hesitation. One cheek bulging, she blew the smoke slowly out of that corner of her mouth.

"Dying man? What are you talking about? Who's dying?"

"Me. Ain't I?"

"Is that what Dr. Dundee told you, Bob?"

"No — that's what he told you. Must have, Een."

She removed her shoulder from the wall and sat down.

"What in hell are you talking about?"

"How much longer did he say I had? How much time? You can come clean with me, Een."

She gave her head a dazed shake, blinking. "Will you run through that again please?"

Now Swirling rose. "I might as well tell you. I saw that — eulogy you've been working on. And before we go any farther with this, I want you to know it's the sweetest thing I've ever . . . I felt all —" He pantomimed "all choked up," then dropped his hands as though overcome with emotion. "And then your trying to tell me without saying so in so many words that you wouldn't, you know, 'mind' if I had an interest in Becky. And *still* a man has these damn, damn guilt feelings!"

"Wait a minute. Let's back this merry-go-round up a little. Eulogy of who?"

"Me. Who else?"

"I really don't get this."

He turned to face her. "I was going through your desk some weeks ago and stumbled on what you've been writing. Or were at the time. Enid —"

"What in *hell* is this all about? Do you remember something of what you saw? That I was writing?"

"Yes." He thought a moment, gazing upwards. "Something about how we're all on loan to one another, and then, oh yes, on this brief day of sun and frost, that lovely line from Walter Pater. No, that's not it. Um, this short day of frost and sun. That's it."

Her face was blank.

"And now the loan is being foreclosed."

His words had been clearly enough understood but would require a moment to be converted into belief. They were like a photographic negative that had to be developed. And indeed the interval before she answered seemed about the length of time it would take a Polaroid SX-70 to extrude its finished picture.

"Jesus Christ! That was a letter of sympathy I was writing to Susan Sharkey when Fred died."

"Wow. Whew. That's a load off my mind."

Swirling quickly sensed, however, that any feeling of relief would be short-lived, if not illusory. The vehemence of Enid's response made that clear.

"You mean to tell me you thought I'd do a thing like that? Actually start preparing your — even before you were —" She gave up with a toss of her arms, as though aware herself that she was beginning to sound like Becky Tingle.

"Don't take it that way. I thought it perfectly understandable in the circumstances." He shook his head with a smile, and made an attempt to direct the now fully recognized shambles into humorous channels. "Six months from now we'll be laughing at this."

Enid's manner made it darkly unlikely that this would ever fall into perspective as a merry marital mix-up in a television sitcom, even in retrospect.

"The kicking up your heels a little while time remained — Oh, Christ, 'while time remained,' she says. That part I don't mind too much. I've given evidence that I was reasonable about your little caper without knowing this *danse macabre* twist you suddenly give it. But that you do it while calmly thinking that here is a wife who can't wait . . ." She gave up again, speechless.

"I tell you I didn't look at it that way. I saw nothing basically wrong with it, and if I didn't, why should you?"

"Because of what it implied you think of me." She rose and walked the room, drawing steadily on the cigar. Each was waiting for the other to go on. Swirling spoke at last.

"Oh, come on. Try to think of it *in my light*. You must, or we're in a quagmire. When it hit me, I, I understood. I forgave you."

Enid wheeled.

"You *forgave* me. There! That proves you thought I was

doing something quite uncalled for. You didn't put it past me."

"No, no!"

He'd known the word was a fatal blunder even as he uttered it. He had once seen a film short of an eminent conductor in the throes of rehearsing *The Firebird* in an outdoor band shell, who at one point broke short the orchestra's rendition of a certain tricky passage by not only rapping on the stand with his baton while crying aloud, but flailing the air with both arms, his head down, as though fighting off a swarm of hornets. Swirling similarly now disclaimed the word, tried to strike it from the record, in order that they might "take it again" from the opening of the tricky passage they were likewise trying to negotiate (though the metaphor of shooting a treacherous rapids might more aptly have suited the case). But there the parallel ended. The word couldn't be struck from the record, a fresh start made with its memory expunged, forgotten like a blue note from the oboes or a momentary infelicitous stridency among the second violins. He had blurted it, and it would haunt any discussion of the subject forever; indeed dictate its course.

"It proves you not only accuse me of doing something wrong, but of something I wasn't even doing."

"So? You didn't do it. That's that."

"No, let me finish. Something I didn't do but you thought me capable of. You didn't put it past me. That's what you think of me."

"Maaw." He bleated it toward the ceiling like a stricken sheep. It was hopeless. And in her reaction she was generating resentment about the Becky business as well, recanting her tolerance about that. The two would become inseparably amalgamated in her emotions, the one feeding the other, so that she herself would probably not know which she was protesting. His guilt in the one was part and parcel of his guilt in the other. His contention now was with the Irishspitfire half of her divided heritage, not the reasonable En-glishwoman noted for her *sang-froid*.

"It's probably the masculine share in the sex war subconsciously twisted and reversed so as to pin the hostility on the woman: *she wishes me dead.*"

"Maaaw." Not that again. His tongue was once more like a shred of rotted fabric, with which he could only manage to bring out the words: "I'm going to kill myself."

"You do that."

If this was to be, then, as now seemed, another skirmish in the War Between the Sexes, he knew his course. He was going AWOL. He strolled to the bar and asked listlessly, "How else was your day? Do you think you'll buy the house?"

"Yes. Do you think you'd like to rent it?"

That Enid may not have been altogether kidding, that that was precisely the irony toward which they were propelled, became ominously more apparent in the days and then weeks that followed. They didn't make love and they didn't make love. He saw that he would not be forgiven for forgiving her. Neither seemed capable of essaying the burden of reconciliation, that first dead weight someone has to pick up. A spiked portcullis lowered between them could not more thoroughly have severed them physically. She knew that when he went out it was probably to see Becky, on whose pleasures and comforts he was increasingly thrown. Enid, too, went out alone, and finally she told him she had been seeing Leo Ludlow, known to have more than a passing interest in her. He and his wife were splitting up, not necessarily over Enid, any more than Swirling's estrangement was solely over Becky. Marriage to Becky was something he boggled at, and he decided to tell her in so many words that it wasn't in the cards. His plan was to lay it on the line one night when they drove to the beach near where they'd first

84

parked, to talk things over. She introduced a rather unexpected element into the discussion before he had got very far with his end of it.

"The thing is, I don't know how long I've got," she said.

"Got?"

"To live."

"What are you talking about?"

"I thought you knew. It was one reason why I wasn't going to deny myself anything, pass up the good times I knew there'd be for us, even for a little while. Live life to the hilt while you've got it."

"You mean no man knows his mortal hour, and so on," he said, gazing out his window and trying not to believe the testimony of his senses, or even that this conversation was taking place.

"A little more than that."

"We only go through this world once sort of thing," he persisted, doggedly resolved that this be given a generalized interpretation.

She pushed in the dashboard lighter and waited for it to pop, a cigarette in her mouth. She lit it and returned the lighter to its socket. She laughed, shaking her head.

"This is going to be weird, or sound weird to you. You know those darling sweet things you say? Calling them blancmanges and all? Well, do you know what the doctors call it when you have a lot of those little nubs in there? Medical jargon. They call it tapioca."

"But they don't think tapioca calls for surgery?"

"Not unless some of them get the idea they want to be oatmeal. We girls just sweat these things out and hope for the best. But what I mean is, don't think you owe me anything in the way of — I mean it's not as though it were your problem. I just wanted you to know what figured in my, um, motivation, but then to say you're not to feel you're under any moral obligation to me. What. So. Ever, Bobolink. You're free as a bird." She darted a glance at him and then quickly looked off toward the chuckling water, with what he hated himself for recognizing as feminine craft. "I mean you're under no obligation to marry me, is what I mean. If you feel you'd even rather break this off, why, fine."

"Of course I'll marry you," he said.

"No sweat?"

"No sweat," he said, reaching into a pocket for his handkerchief.

Six

ENID WAS GENEROUS-minded in settlement. Disdaining alimony, she also rented the house to the newlyweds for four hundred dollars a month, which Swirling promised to increase the moment his finances looked up, or Becky began to earn a little more herself selling properties such as this. That was a hundred and fifty dollars less than Enid had been getting from her first tenants, who asked to be freed of their lease just when the divorce came through. Becky's remarriage put an end to her own modest alimony, but her mother helped her out from time to time. Once widowed and once divorced herself (from the father of Becky's stepbrother Pomfret) she was now "married to a man with a cigar in his mouth," as Becky put it.

For a wedding present the fabled Pomfret sent the Swirlings an indoor swing. It was in the form of a wicker basket chair with two chains ending in grappling hooks by means of which it could be hung in any doorway, suspended from the lintel molding. Becky was swinging in and out of the living room one evening after dinner, propelling herself back and forth with the toe of her shoe, as Swirling unpacked books and alphabetized them on the shelves. She smiled as she contemplated the furnishing and decorating they had already done.

"We'd better get those draperies up before Pomfret gets here."

"Gets here?" he asked, on his knees and over his shoulder.

"Didn't I tell you he's coming for a short visit? He won't like them one little bit."

"Why not?"

"He'll think them too busy. He thinks everything is too busy."

That was more than could be said for Pomfret, who apparently hadn't held a job within living memory. Except for one- or two-week cabaret engagements as an extemporaneous poet. He claimed to be the only one in the country. After a few such gigs he would revert to considering the lilies. Swirling was eager to meet this rumored *rara avis*, but not as eager as he would be to see his back once he got here. That he knew in his bones in advance.

Pomfret himself gave the illusion of not having any bones. He was first seen sagging under the weight of three bags, one in each hand and one under his arm, in addition to a shoulder bag, as he came up the walk to the house after climbing out of a cab. He was wearing banana boots, clam diggers, the upper half of a blue denim leisure suit, and a French engineer's cap. Watching from a window upstairs, Swirling had seen quite enough: his brother-in-law could go now. But the quantity of luggage boded ill, as though its owner had never heard of the Oriental proverb about guests and fish after three days.

"Pom!" Becky flew up the walk to embrace him. "And you've brought Mrs. Gluckstern!" That would be the basset who waddled into the house, her great dugs grazing the threshold. An enormous reluctance kept Swirling rooted to the landing above. It seemed to overpower him from the feet up, a familiar sensation when coping with the unpreferred, like getting wet with your clothes on, so that he felt as though he were growing heavier with each step as he finally began the grim descent. He seemed to weigh a quarter of a ton by the time he reached the vestibule. By that time the bags had been dropped there, and the other two had gone on into the living room in a spate of exchanged exclamation. He stood there listening to them a moment longer, sincerely trying to pluck up the spirit to greet his brother-in-law hospitably, give him a cheerful welcome. He delayed just a moment longer. Pomfret was talking about his doctor, a brilliant man who had finally tracked down the allergy from which he had been suffering when last seen. "It's a grass called fescue found in most lawns. Why nobody else could identify the villain I don't know, I thought for a while it might be Mrs. Gluckstern, but no. Dr. Bromley loves pricking people for those sensitivity tests, so it was no surprise to me to find he's bonkers over acupuncture. Studying it to practice it. Actually, politically he's a Maoist."

"That's the chink in his armor?" Swirling said, entering with his Groucho stride and flirting an imaginary cigar.

"Hm?"

"Pom, this is Bob," Becky said. "Bob, Pomfret."

Swirling hadn't been prepared for any resemblance between Becky and Pomfret since they weren't blood relatives, just stepchildren united in childhood by the marriage of her divorced mother to his widowed father, but there was some. They were both fair and gray-eyed, and both under medium height. But the marked similarity lay in their gestures and general mode of speech. They both waved their hands in all directions when they talked, both raised their eyebrows to emphasize words, as though to italicize them. Similarities of children to parents and to each other are as often the result of imitation as inheritance, and Swirling had a hunch that some of Becky's mannerisms likewise resulted from an early habit of unconsciously imitating a slightly older brother clearly considered the cat's whiskers. But there was one major difference. Pomfret spoke in sentences that parsed. And he would deliver himself sententiously on any subject, whether asked or not.

His range of interests was amazingly broad. He loved music ("Mahler tells me that it's a quarter to twelve."); art ("*The Night Watch* is eleven inches too wide."); food ("There are few things more degrading to the human spirit than Brussels sprouts."); the theater ("With a little more work out of town this could have been whipped into a bit of inconsequential fluff."); wine ("Take this back and tell the sommelier to bring us a six-pack of Schlitz."); literature ("There is nothing for fiction to do but return to narrative, just as there is nothing for a drunk to do but go home."); psychoanalysis ("A persistent appetite for cold cuts is almost certainly indicative of latent necrophilia."). His unsleeping vivisection of friends and acquaintances was an urge he would be the first to admit might have constructions put on it. "Your idiosyncrasy, Bob," he said to Swirling one night, "that habit you have of always keeping a cigarette firm and fully packed by pressing the end hard with your thumb between puffs, has obviously phallic overtones."

"But I don't smoke cigarettes."

"That's what you think."

His stated tenet, that only will-o'-the-wisps were worth pursuing, was one on which Swirling wished he would act, because after three weeks he still seemed to have no immediate plans for departure. He read aloud Auden's praise of the vertical man while lying stretched out horizontally on the sofa one night. Becky swung to and fro in the doorway and beamed. She adored Pom, and often smiled in Swirling's direction, sharing with him their good luck in having Pomfret around. Pomfret was one of those people who know how to live. Swirling kept hinting that even brief intervals of employment would net him enough to take some more trips, for Pomfret loved to travel. ("Albania smells like burnt rubber.")

"What would you like to do more than anything else in the world, Pomfret?" Swirling asked him one evening when they were on their way to dinner at a country restaurant.

"Make love on a bed of steamed rice."

"No, I meant in the sense of, well, real action." The awful word must be uttered. "A job."

"I would like to be one of those men who go around to public places and decide on the number of people occupancy by more than which is dangerous and unlawful. Where is this restaurant?"

"About ten or twelve more miles to go."

"Oh, good. Fourteen miles is the ideal distance to drive to dinner. I see you're wearing those opal earrings I love, Becky. Opals always put an edge on my appetite."

Swirling was gripping the steering wheel as though he was going to tear it off and throw it out the window. Becky turned around and began to recall for Pomfret, who was sitting in the back seat, the time when as a little girl she and a couple of friends had been playing grown-up, and had not only put on her mother's dress and slippers, but had bedecked herself with all the jewels she could lay her hands on. The reference to the opals had touched off the reminiscence.

"Mother was absolutely pale when she — I mean her real jewels, I carted the whole chest from her dresser out to where we were — it was in the garden, that was thick with that wild flower that you said started your hay fever — something-me-not — not forget-me-not — oh, what was the name of that yellow blossom it had? Touch-me-not, that's it. Well, when Mother realized what I had on, her best pearls, her diamond brooch —"

Swirling had a sudden flash of insight into Becky's conversational style. She was a Cubist, breaking up sentences and geometrically reassembling their grammatical components, as artists did linear, those that had subjects being denied predicates, or having them crop up elsewhere in the design, while predicates stood juxtaposed in artful divorce from their subjects. What applied to sentences did to words as well; they too were systematically fragmented and rearranged in the general canvas. The canvas was the paragraph, and there was a compositional entity despite what was said by the uninitiated who found the total baffling, or those unschooled in the sort of thing she was trying to do, and which Swirling himself now found charming. Thus what seemed at first blush verbosity was in fact extreme concision. Words gave the effect of being prodigally squandered while in fact few were wasted.

Reminiscences lasted them till they reached the restaurant, a large remodeled mansion where good French food was said to be served. They relinquished the car to a parking attendant and went in. As they followed the captain into the dining room, Pomfret paused to look at a mural, a large waterscape done by an artist who had taken a good look at Dufy. They all stopped with him and waited, sensing that comment was imminent. Even the captain stood respectfully by for the verdict.

"The murals in restaurants are on a par with the food in museums," Pomfret stated. The captain nodded, smiling, and resumed escorting them to their table. Swirling spotted the generalization as not only having been stored up in advance, for impromptu delivery when the occasion arose, but also as reversible, like a raglan that could double as a raincoat by being turned inside out. He could see them all already, lunching on tuna fish at the Guggenheim while Pomfret murmured, "The food in museums . . ."

Over drinks, Pomfret was pressed for his views on religion,

not especially by Swirling. Asked whether he believed in an afterlife, he said, "Yes. This is it. That's what those intimations of previous incarnations are all about."

As he jabbered on, Swirling's mind wandered back to an incident with his own younger sister, Eleanor, now these many years gone. As an adolescent (defined by Pomfret as "a vat of boiling hormones") he had rebelled against his family's rigid fundamentalism. He could recall his holding forth to an assemblage of aunts and uncles one Sunday afternoon, denying, not only immortality, but that man had any such thing as a soul at all. "Created by God, a little lower than the angels? Rubbish. Man is just another biological happenstance. I don't consider myself a little lower than the angels at all. I'm just a bit of organic scum infesting the outer crust of one of the lesser planets." "He's so stuck-up," Eleanor had said. Swirling smiled at the memory, in time for Pomfret to think it was in response to something he'd just said about women, a subject on which he was a mine of *obiter dicta*.

"Do you think you'll marry, Pomfret?" Swirling asked.

"No."

"Why not?" Swirling went on, suddenly inspired to play the clod. He deliberately avoided Becky's quizzical gaze.

"I don't like pushing things."

"What do you mean?"

"Husbands are always pushing things, it's the story of their lives. Supermarket carts, perambulators, lawn mowers, grass fertilizers, wheelbarrows. Name it, and a husband will be pushing it."

The arrival of the check found Pomfret engrossed in the murals, having evidently found merit in them after all, enough to warrant pondering details of their composition until the business at hand had been completed.

But none could say he didn't sing for his supper. When they were home again in the studio living room, he did his regular nightcap, a mock news roundup he called the Eleven O'Clock Wrap-up, which was based on a routine he had experimentally toyed with in his nightclub stints.

"Good evening," he said, using a candlestick for a microphone, "this is Gordon Poonsnatcher substituting for Lionel Tuftfondler on your Eleven O'Clock Wrap-up. Attempts to reach an agreement in the threatened corset-stay-inserters' strike have again collapsed. Both sides were pessimistic as they left the mediation room. 'The universe is apparently without meaning,' the president of the corset-stay-inserters' union, a collector of Beckett first editions, was heard to say. 'Yes, life is a fortuitous concatenation of atoms,' an officer of the Bodice Buddy Corporation agreed. The contagious gloom has spread to the entire garment district, where people were heard dejectedly mouthing similar Existentialist truisms ... Harlow Twitchell has announced his candidacy for President on the Surrealist ticket. 'My campaign will be different,' he declared in a policy statement issued early today. 'Instead of going around the country eating barbecued ribs and wearing ten-gallon hats, I shall eat ten-gallon hats and wear barbecued ribs. My Virginia estate, Non Sequitur, will be our second White House, and there I shall meet regularly with trusted advisers in a full and open exchange of our dreams. Until this country shall have a new birth of freedom, Caesarean if necessary' ... Avalon, Connecticut. A decadent coterie of sex deviants was raided early this evening at their regular meeting place, the home of Mr. Robert Swirling, 718 Benson Road. Swirling, a debonair flagellant known as Cool Whip, was released on one thousand dollars' bail after he was arrested and booked on a charge of violating the Corrupt Practices Act. A landmark decision is anticipated if the case ..."

Swirling knew the exact moment when he was going bananas. Not the precise point in time as such, but the cue word with which Pomfret would trip his responses and send him amok.

Hardest to bear were Pomfret's English affectations. Called to the phone, he would say, "Pomfret here," or he would himself ring so-and-so up rather than give him a buzz, which sufficed most of his fellow Americans. He said "in due course" (if not, indeed, "in jew course") and that he "hadn't got" something, and also he spoke of giving people lunch instead of taking them to it. Sometime, none could tell when, but inevitably sometime, lying stretched out on the couch, Pomfret would be reading the Conrail timetable in connection with a trip into the city. Or he would have some other occasion to say "schedule." And he would give it the British fricative instead of the good old time-honored and perfectly serviceable American glottal. He would say "shedule." And Swirling would spring into action.

Having ripped the unapproved draperies from their moorings, he would then with maniacal leisure tear them into longitudinal strips suitable for binding Pomfret as well as lashing him to the sofa. Pomfret would not be gagged. A more conclusive measure must be taken. Swirling would climb aboard his prey, laughing shrilly as he straddled him at about torso level, shove the nozzle of a vacuum cleaner down his throat, and flip the switch. All of Pomfret's insides would thus be sucked upward into the receptacle sack. Uh-fuh-dee, uh-fuh-dee, uh that's all folks! A bag of giblets. Yes, siree. No ifs, ands or buts. Just an easily closeable conveniently disposable bag . . . of . . . guts!

Why the rhymes? Because that was Pomfret's professed line of country, the one conceivable means by which he might be nudged out of one's hair and back into gainful employment. Back to the hungry i on the Coast, the Dull Roar in Chicago — anywhere. Pomfret was an extemporaneous poet, one heard, did one not? That was his cabaret act.

Tippling patrons would send up scraps of information about themselves, their names, hometowns, occupations, anything, and from such scribbled data Pomfret would take the spotlight and weave his impromptu verses, just the way pianists — such as the well-remembered Alec Templeton — would concoct a fugue from popular songs suggested by the audience. One heard that his dash-offs were pretty good too, allowing for their being of the Ogden Nash couplet kind with the long windup affording time to think out and pitch the mating rhyme.

Peeping at Becky and Pomfret over his evening paper, wondering how he had ever got into this, as if he didn't know, Swirling often also wondered whether it ever occurred to the cliché-abhorring Pomfret that he had them locked into the bromide of all time: the brother-in-law who doesn't work. Well, Swirling was going to do something about that on the above lines, and he did, and things did get better. But not, of course, before they got worse.

Swirling was eating a late breakfast one Saturday morning while Becky was out showing houses when Pomfret sort of slithered down the stairs in his pajamas, like a large blob of mercury, one hand sliding along the banister while the other clutched his chest. "I can hardly breathe," he said, and the croaking wheeze with which he brought the words out certainly corroborated them. Swirling's laugh was the kind by which we often involuntarily express sympathy in another's plight. "I'm dying . . ." Swirling dropped his coffee and ran excitedly up the stairs for the thermometer, passing Pomfret on the way with a "steady on" squeeze of his shoulder. But Pomfret had no temperature, then or the days following, which offered no signs of improvement. The trouble was a deep chest congestion, not amenable to antibiotics, for which there was only one solution. "Get the humidity in the house up, up, up," Dr. Dundee said, with an air of making a set speech of which he was himself weary. "Air dried by constant furnace heat is one of the banes of modern living, and the cause for more respiratory and sinus ailments than you can shake a stick at, shake a stick at, shake a stick at." Pretending he was a cracked phonograph record was his way of saying that he was giving monotonously obvious annual advice to which people were, monotonously, unresponsive. "Get some humidifiers going here — I'll bet the humidity's down to ten — get those plumes of vapor going is all I can tell you. These sensations that he's dying are the result of inflammation momentarily closing the larynx when he, literally, can't breathe. But there's nothing to be afraid of. If we faint, it all automatically starts up again. There's no danger, no danger, no danger."

Not to Pomfret. The eight or ten humidifiers hissing away everywhere in the house gradually relieved his asthmatic symptoms but sent Swirling back to an amateur repairman's manual entitled *First Aid for the Ailing House,* to see what might be done to stave off the seemingly inevitable disintegration of his property — or rather Enid's property — due to damp rot. The paper peeled off the walls; paneling began to blister; ceilings cracked and flaked, dropping bits of plaster here and there like a kind of gently but steadily descending domestic dandruff. Mildew appeared on books, on clothing, on furniture. The *mildew* had mildew. Postage stamps lost their adhesive properties while soda crackers and gingersnaps failed to crepitate when eaten. Forget it. Swirling thought he would not have been surprised to wake up one morning and find his watch hanging over the edge of the bureau top, as in a Dali fantasy. The conceit amused Becky no end. And through the perpetual mists disconsolately wandered Mrs. Gluckstern, her tongue lolling out farther than ever, her great dugs grazing the carpets.

Munching an inaudible cheese chip, as they sat over their cocktails one evening, Swirling debated with himself whether he should suggest it was their duty to go to Enid and apprise her of the swiftening decay of her house. As though in a telepathically timed reproach, Pomfret instituted a coughing fit especially notable in volume and duration. It told them they were by no means out of the woods yet. "Terrible congestion," he said.

"Yes, isn't it," Swirling said drily (!), looking away. Nobody got it. At least the situation was not without its compensations. There were no Eleven O'Clock Wrap-ups. Pom hadn't the strength, or the inclination. But he did continue to brighten their evenings together with bits of conversational tinsel thrown out from the parlor sofa, now an invalid's pallet, on which he lay palely loitering. There was the crackle of non sequiturs, and there were the glacéed absolutes that were his gift to homespun philosophy. "Being an only child, I naturally chewed a lot of gum." "You can't be happy with a woman who's writing a biography of Emanuel Swedenborg." "Hawthorne was a voyeur with myopia." "There are some things, like the spelling of jodhpurs, that can never be made to look right." There were frequent allusive salutes to the masters of preciosity who had gone before, like the well-regarded Ronald Firbank. "He once ate a single pea for dinner. Did you know that?"

"No, I hadn't realized that," Swirling said.

"I mean what's left after that?"

"Nothing much I expect."

There were meandering reminiscences with Becky, who had rescued him from the plight of an only child at age eight, on which Swirling was free to tune in if he were so minded. "You remember Myron Middleton on our block, Sis, who ate mayonnaise out of the jar and wrote cinquains. That's a verse form now no longer practiced," he explained to Swirling, rolling his head on the sofa cushion as he cast an eye in his direction. "What great things we expected of Myron. And has he fulfilled the class prophecy — Pulitzer Prize poet? Well, I ran into him some time ago in New York. He recognized me — I never should have him. Because there was no mistaking what that face had become. It was the face of a participating neighborhood dealer. No need to be told he owned an Oldsmobile agency in Queens. It was writ large in those lineaments. After a brief exchange of gossip, I said, 'I'm taking a crosstown bus here. Can I drop you? . . .'"

Swirling snatched a newspaper up off the floor and began to eat it, or at least did so in mental rehearsal for the time when things Would Come to Such a Pass. That would be it, for him, marbles-wise. Uh-fuh-dee, uh-fuh-dee, uh that's all folks. Clap the net over him and give him tenure in some local warehouse.

Pomfret called to mind the words of the old hymn, "Art thou weary, are thou languid?" But he promised that with the first sign of returning strength he would fix them all a meal to remember. There would be a prefatory salmon mousse, sent downhill with plenty of young Gewürztraminer. The main course would be a hearty cassoulet, with a burly Chambertin born to stand up to it. Then they would all turn a few handsprings to clear their palates, before sitting down to a lemon soufflé like angel's hair, sipping a chilled Barsac the while, to be sure. Later they might toy with a little Brie. Swirling thought he would tie a small wheel of it to the end of a piece of string, for Pomfret to run it up and down on, like a yo-yo. Swirling sometimes vied valiantly to sustain his end of the talk on a level with the *délicatesses* being dished out; but at the moment all he could think of was an epigram on the wall of his cheesemonger's store. "A meal without cheese is like a kiss without a squeeze," he said, and turned away in an agony of shame. He might as well have said there were good and bad in all races, or that marriage was a give and take — as on some occasions he thought of doing deliberately, in the wild hope of driving Pomfret out of the house and maybe even the country.

A clump of plaster fell from the ceiling just then, a few scraps settling on a book lying on a coffee table. It was a novel Pomfret was reading, with a slice of Swiss cheese in it for a bookmark. Swirling stared at it until his appetite for outrage had been temporarily glutted. Then he returned their collective attention to the flurries from above. Before going to the kitchen for a broom and dustpan, he paused to assess a lengthening crack overhead, stepping over to a spot where he was visible to everybody. He wanted Pomfret to get the point: *that the plaster was falling,* prefiguring the time when the whole house must come apart and bury them all in rubble, like Samson and the Philistines in the temple. But Pomfret only went on lying there looking curiously weightless and insubstantial, like a Christ just lifted down from the cross in a painting of the Crucifixion. How could anyone who looked like that utter sentences with bits of citron in them?

He propped the broom and dustpan against the wall when he had finished sweeping up, took a sip of his drink, and said, "Well, I must get to my books." He excused himself to fetch a damp cloth and resume wiping mildew from his library where he had left off the evening before, among the L's, with a treasured uniform five-volume edition of Ring Lardner.

Then there was an unexpected ray of light, thanks to a fresh turn of events that dramatized the impossibility of the situation. Swirling developed a chest congestion. Evidently the damp air was as bad for him as the dry was for Pomfret. He developed a hacking cough, which he speedily learned to graduate in volume and length whenever there was anyone in earshot, with a virtuosity that threatened to outclass the competition. The dragged step, the hunched posture, the ubiquitous Kleenex box, all these must certainly make it clear that the house wasn't big enough for both of them. Yet they didn't. Then Swirling had an idea.

It hit him all of a heap as he was washing some upper

windows. He'd had to go down cellar for the squeegee, and it was odd the notion hadn't occurred to him there. It was when he was again at work on the windows that the inspiration struck him. Of course! Pomfret must be cajoled into the basement. The atmospheric conditions they'd spent hundreds of dollars in appliances to obtain through the house prevailed there all the time. They were ideal *without* humidifiers. A humidity gauge he left there for an hour proved it. The reading remained precisely the same as it had upstairs — a perfect 53.

It was while driving to the supermarket with Becky the following evening that he proposed his solution. "A bed in the front corner, a few comfortable chairs, a desk, some rugs, and lamps, and presto, a snug little room with just the right conditions . . ."

He could sense from Becky's silence that this was not going down at all well. But there was nothing to do but push on.

"Some beaverboard or plywood could easily be thrown up to screen off the furnace and junk section of the cellar . . ."

"You mean you'd put Pomfret down in the basement?"

The response was such that Swirling quickly changed his line.

"No, no, of course not. I mean that *I* could move down there. For nights I mean. With some *de*humidifiers. Don't you see? It will solve all our problems."

She was hugging his arm with both of hers, her head on his shoulder, as though saying she could hardly believe her luck. She was congratulating herself on the jewel she had snared. "What, *what* a love."

But she wouldn't hear of it. Spring was only a month away, and that would solve their problems. They would vanish the first day the furnace was off. There was another call on his magnanimity.

"We have this third bill from the doctor's office, and since

Pom doesn't have the money just now, and we both hate being dunned, and I'm on the verge of closing that terrific Bascom estate deal, so it'd not be any skin off your — and just a loan of course. Bobolink, are you going to hit the ceiling?"

"That shouldn't be too hard. Most of it is on the floor."

It was at times like this that he felt himself a little overshriven, as though he had now not only paid for his sins but had a fat moral balance to his credit, on which he might draw, as it were, for another fling.

He could not have imagined with whom. Nor that Enid and Becky between them would be the unwitting instruments for bringing it about. Yes. He was going to live if it killed him.

Seven

"Killing time, Pomfret?"

"Only in self-defense."

Swirling made a face by opening his mouth and then snapping his jaws shut again, like a dog biting a fly out of the air.

It was spring.

"I've got a job for you," he said, taking a menacing step forward. He was going to lay it on the line. Since this was to be a direct confrontation, he stood behind and a little to the left of the figure stretched out on the sofa, the top of its towhead just visible above a tussock of cushions propped against one arm, on a level with the stocking feet crossed on the other.

"Oh?"

"Yes. You remember that American Express freight office we saw coming slowly toward us up the street a while ago? They've eliminated the branch here in town, as they are with so many, and so somebody bought the building, or maybe got it for the hauling away. He moved it to a vacant lot he owns on River Road. That somebody turns out to be Dick Jacquemoux, a guy I know slightly. It's Enid who really does. That's my ex-wife you'll remember. She's called Enid Ludlow now." Why had he adopted one of Pomfret's fake Anglicisms? Why couldn't he just have said she was named that, or that was her name now? "I ran into her the other day and we had some cocoa together. Well, over this cocoa I got the dope on what's to become of that American Express freight office. Jacquemoux is converting it into a supper cabaret!"

The stocking feet at the other end of the sofa rubbed against each other, like awful creatures, while a hand made some adjustments in the hummock of cushions on the nearer end. Go on.

Swirling took a step to the left and one forward. His manner became more threatening.

"It'll be a kind of in-the-round café, with singing, instrumental and comedy acts. You know the sort of thing. Well, I asked Enid to speak to him about you, and he responded very favorably to booking your act in. He's looking for talent, in fact scraping the — So it's no more being bored and restless around here, physical ailments emotional in origin, empty shell, stuck on dead center, but a chance to get cracking again. Not drinking too much because we're at loose ends, and hate ourselves. No. Wind in our sails and it's off and away! What do you say to that, eh, Pom?"

"I mustn't listen to a word you say, dear boy, or I shall become prey to wholesome thoughts."

Swirling bit another fly out of the air, his teeth clicking together audibly this time, provoking a twang from a worrisome incisor, while his eyes besought heaven.

"Remodeling's almost completed," he forged implacably on, "in fact Jacquemoux wants to open *as soon as he can get a show together*. He already has that folksinger who calls herself the Miller's Daughter. The one who can sit on her hair and accompanies herself on the zither. Then a local jazz group who are no slouches either. Really slap-up stuff. Cut two platters already. And then there's you. The novelty act he needs to round out a really good variety card. April's here, your health is much better, mine too for that matter, so things are looking up again, what, Pompon?"

Pompon said nothing for a moment. He'd been reading a book, which now at least lay spread-eagled on his stomach. Swirling pressed his advantage. He stepped smartly forward two more steps and turned, in order that Pomfret could see him squarely now, and, seeing him, realize that he was firm about this and meant business. This was a showdown. "The place will be called the Nosebag," he said, "and after a success there it's no telling how far you'll go. The right agent could shoot you straight across the country, which is full of this kind of experimental café springing up everywhere."

"Why are they calling it the Nosebag?"

"Antiglamour, current mood of. Inverted snobbishness, example of, with a little nostalgia thrown in. Big thing these days. 'Let's put on the nosebag,' people used to say in my cawntree. The raunchy nuance, the exquisite throwaway, that's the angle now. *C'est le temps*. There's a comedian loose in the countryside who calls himself the Pile of Crud. Well, you'll show him a thing or two! Won't you just!"

Pomfret took to it like a duck to bigarade sauce. Not that he openly showed it. But beneath the surface air of mere acquiescence could be detected a secret eagerness to take the spotlight again. Since the act was impromptu there was no question of "auditioning" for Jacquemoux. But Jacquemoux had heard of this extemporizer, and the reports had been favorable. The agreement made was that Pomfret's first performance would be his audition, and if suitable, he would be hired for an engagement, payment to include that initial stint.

Doing his turn off the cuff eliminated the toils of preparation, but the anxiety of approaching performance time was equivalently more anguished. As the hour drew near for going on cold, with nothing in hand, before yet another unpredictable audience, Pomfret's tension became intolerable — even to those around him enduring the fallout. His nerves were a can of worms, his stomach a cavern of bats, his head threatening to split open. Inside it the Budapest String Quartet were sawing away, each at a different composition. Becky did her best to soothe or distract him, holding his hand, stroking his neck, massaging his back. "Why don't you, not cheat a little, just cook up a few zingers in advance. You know a *few* of the people who'll be there opening night," she reminded him as she administered an alcohol rub where he lay prone on the couch, stripped to the waist, his face mangled against the cushions. Watching sympathetically from the swing, Swirling agreed. But that was no soap. It would be *infra dig*, a breach of the code. As Robert Frost preferred having his comments about his poetry "wrung from him" by the audience questions following his public readings, so Pomfret Stiles would have his verses wrung from him in the pressure of the moment. He would do as he was billed. He extemporized poetry, like Cyrano de Bergerac.

His first show was to be at nine o'clock on the Saturday night of the Grand Opening, and the Nosebag was crowded to capacity. They had known for a day or so that it would be, from Dick Jacquemoux's report on the reservations pouring in. It would be a sellout. Pomfret's nerves were now like violin strings which the Budapest String Quartet ensemblists were tightening to the snapping point by twisting the pegs located inside his head. He had the conviction that his neck was that of one of the violins. He could not go on; he would kill himself. After a sketchy supper at home, Becky walked him around the back yard, like a nervous racehorse before post time. From one of the casement windows, of traumatic memory, Swirling watched the two mystic figures tramping steadily in the gathering dusk. Downstairs Mrs. Gluckstern could be heard hurrying from room to room looking for her hidden tennis ball, planted somewhere in a game she liked to play and that Pomfret liked to play with her. It was one of his forms of relaxation, partial at least. He would hide the ball and then let her hunt for it, rooting under chair cushions, pawing about behind tables, and creeping and scrabbling under the skirts of sofa upholstery or among the objects in the kitchen broom closet.

At last it came time to gird their loins and set out for the Nosebag. Mrs. Gluckstern had found the tennis ball — in a space between the icebox and the electric range — and to keep her happily occupied in their absence Pomfret hid it again, as she wished. After looking about for a new spot, he finally dropped it into a galosh on the floor of the vestibule closet, Swirling holding her forcibly in the kitchen till he had done so.

The cabaret was nearly full when they got there, most of the patrons finishing a seven-thirty or eight o'clock dinner. Restoration and remodeling had been restricted to what a city building inspector had insisted on for safety, so that the outside and inside both bore reminders of the American Express freight shed it had once been. Old theatrical and circus posters hung on the walls contributed to the note of nostalgia. Tables with red-and-white-checked cloths and napkins concentrically circled a round dais in the middle of the barn, with space allowed for dancing. The four-piece band was belting out middle-of-the-road jazz, though they called themselves the Left of Center. Perhaps efforts of a more enterprising kind would come later. At the moment a half-dozen people were dancing to "Milenberg Joy." At one end was a small bar for those not intending to sup. Near it, three tables had been pushed together into one long one, and as Swirling and his party entered, he saw Dick Jacquemoux standing at the head of it waving them vehemently over. They were to sit with him, as his guests. Tall, with a positive bonfire of wild red hair, he could hardly have been missed, even across the gathering hubbub of patrons and waiters. "I'm going home," Pomfret said. "My feet are coming off." Steering him firmly forward by the elbow, Swirling noted other cause for dismay. His heart sank at the sight he might have expected to see. Enid and Leo Ludlow were firmly established as part of Jacquemoux's party.

Two men who have shared a woman, let alone as wife, are bound to find any encounter constraining, full of uneasy overtones and undertones, sticky suspicions that the woman herself must secretly and perhaps even openly compare them as mates. Two factors qualified such embarrassment for Swirling. Trafficking in any such confidences would be beneath Enid. And Leo was openly good-natured, what you'd call a swell egg. At forty-something, he was getting a bit hefty amidships, and reddening features bore out rumors that he drank too much. Swirling shook hands heartily, trying to generate relaxation by simulating it, as a school of psychologists advises. After a flurry of greeting Swirling suggested he and Leo go to the bar and fetch everyone drinks, the waiters being desperately busy just then. They had a quick whiskey together while the barman filled the other orders.

"I was just recalling the last time we met," Leo said as they hunched over their glasses. "At Ed Cogshell's, when he was still married to Marie, Charlie Tingle was still married to Becky — Do you mind?"

"Push on."

"It was the damnedest thing. You remember that argument that came out of nowhere, about testicles?" Leo laughed, shaking his head.

"You know," Swirling said, leaning an elbow on the bar as he turned to face Leo, "that has its counterpart in women's breasts. Fact. One of them is lower than the other too. Or higher, if you want to take the quixotic view."

Leo was shaking his head. He sucked at his glass and said, "No. I thought that too, till I made a point of researching the matter more closely. Can be done with impunity on any city street now. It's not that at all, begging your pardon, old boy, et cetera, et cetera. One whole *side* is lower than the other. One *shoulder*. Same as a man, as your tailor knows every time he fits you for a coat. A woman — look at them closely — a woman even *leans* to one side or the other. Lists to port or starboard. Shoulders on a level? Not one in a thousand. And I'll tell you something else I've noticed — one of these little obsessions that come and go, leaving scarcely a trace. A woman will always carry her bag on the higher shoulder. Sort of instinctive. Unconscious you might say. She may not even be aware of the reason, to wit that it'd slide off the other."

Swirling's sense of deflation, while not in degree as bad as that experienced at the polo match in regard to how the ball was struck with the mallet, was nevertheless similar in kind. So he had observed nothing. He saw nothing — not even what he was looking straight at. It took a cost account executive like Leo Ludlow to display that first rudimentary endowment of the artist that Swirling so abysmally lacked: power of observation.

He paid for their two drinks, ordered two more, and carried them to the table together with the rest, using a tray. Under the swelling din of the cabaret Swirling had a moment to put his head together with Enid about some remaining undivided possessions, mainly a painting. The problem as always was especially acute in the case of what had been come by as wedding presents.

The painting had been given them by a Chicago cousin of Swirling's who had picked it up for peanuts from a friend who owed him some money; for the amount of the debt in fact, a hundred dollars, which the cousin had written off anyway. It was a still life by the Russian Expressionist Jaw-lensky, of whom the cousin had never heard, and of whom he learned nothing but that he was one of a group called the Blue Four — the one who hadn't caught on as Klee, Feininger and Kandinsky, the other three, had. At least not then. He hadn't really liked the still life, and neither, truth to tell, had the newlyweds, who hung it in unfavored corners of the house when it wasn't stored in the attic. Now Swirling and Becky were "trying it" in the studio living room.

"Look, I don't feel right about taking it," Swirling told Enid against the noise of the band. "Jawlensky's a late bloomer, but coming into his own. I'm sure it's worth a few thousand dollars now — if not several. Shall we just sell it and divide the money?"

"Forget it," Enid said, a little impatiently. "We agreed to split up things like that according to family. That came from yours. Some of the heirlooms from mine are valuable too. Those Tiffany vases are fetching fabulous prices now. The show's about to start."

A prolonged crashing chord from the band served as a gavel rap summoning the house to order. The piano player served as emcee. He took the mike and introduced the Miller's Daughter. Pomfret was to be sandwiched in between her and a ramble comic. Seated on a stool in a simple blue frock, her sheaf of long gold hair gleaming in the spotlight, she plucked a zither and sang "Widdicomb Fair," "Molly Malone," "Foggy, Foggy Dew" and several other folk songs. Her sweet voice earned her two encores, and then she withdrew. Jacquemoux waved her over to his table, where she sat down in the chair vacated by Pomfret.

Pomfret, his nerves apparently under control now that he was on, briefly laid the groundwork for his stunt. Waiters would pass out paper and pencil to the customers, who were then to jot down what they wished about themselves, or might deem of interest to the troubadour. They would also please rise and read off what they had scribbled before turning it in, so he could get a look at them personally. All these preliminaries having been complied with, he began.

"First of all, if we can quiet down the Babel,
Let me give you the dope on the head table.
That flaming heterosexual on the end is our owner and manager,
And not, as you might originally have thought, a scarlet tanager.
The regal lady no doubt fending off his amorous entreaty
Is Mrs. Ludlow, often confused, thanks to that exquisite throat, with Queen Nefertiti.
Then, oh, my God, if it isn't a local character named Robert Swirling.
He has very little character, but what there is is sterling.
His erotic exploits have rocked the community — to sleep.
Still, it ill becomes us to sell the old boy too cheap.
Sitting betwixt his ex-wife and his current
Appears to pose no ostensible deterrent
To flirting with someone he really hadn't oughter —
Namely our delectable songbird, the Miller's Daughter!"

A round of laughter led by the folksinger herself was followed by a ripple of applause. She gave an embarrassed twist of her head, her gold mane swaying along the back of her chair.

"He's broken the ice," Enid whispered to Swirling, who whispered back, "Now let's hope he doesn't fall through it. He's supposed to only get going when he insults people." Enid raised her eyebrows and said, *"Well?"* Swirling shrugged, as though disclaiming any umbrage at the good-natured opening.

Out of the tail of his eye he saw that Becky sat with her head bowed, the fingers of both hands crossed. He didn't dare look at her directly. The anxiety she communicated was so intense he could taste it. His own heart beat faster, and his throat tightened. Under his shirt he could feel rivulets of perspiration trickling. An uneasy silence had fallen on the house. Pomfret was shuffling through his notes at unexpected length. An audience even momentarily lost is an awful dead weight to pick up again, as any entertainer or lecturer knows. A reasonable interval must be allowed for mentally grinding the submitted data into rhymed grain, but when the delay prolonged itself a threat of really acute embarrassment descended on the house. Horror itself was not to be ruled out. "Oh, sheesh," Becky breathed. The click of a cigarette lighter was heard, a woman's whisper, a nervous giggle. "Waiting for a streetcar, Mac?" some lout called from the bar.

Then suddenly Pomfret took off. He fired a smile at his hearers, grasped the mike again, and began pouring out a steady stream of couplets in his not unpleasantly nasal voice — it had the clean stridency of a banjo. Part of the feat was remembering who had said or sent up what, keeping faces matched with details scribbled or called out, so that his performance was in part like that of the memory wizard of vaudeville days. What the Germans called a *Gedächtniskünstler*. He pointed to a man at a ringside table.

"Ladies and gentlemen, that tall bespectacled bird is a research scientist named Cole.
He's so scientific-minded he sends one of his kids to Sunday school and keeps the other one home for control.
Laboratory experimentation was not his first love, for the fact is
Some years ago he was barred from conventional medical practice.
We all make mistakes, but he laid the all-time professional egg

By diagnosing as erysipelas what was really a broken leg.
Will an imminent breakthrough on some experiments of his
 assuage the resulting hypochondriasis?
Yes, siree. He's perfected a pharmaceutical preparation said
 to be a sight for psoriasis.
My own personal hunch is that as an obstetrician he'd make
 a helluva fella.
Because just look at the way he took out that penknife and
 circumcised that panatela."

Without executing a bow of the kind openly soliciting
applause, Pomfret got a good round of it simply by taking a
step back, accompanied by an unobtrusive nod. Those at the
head table discharged their accumulated anxiety by clapping
hysterically, and even giving out with a whistle or two.

As he warmed to this task he became a little bawdy, sailing
pretty close to the wind in one or two cases, notably that of a
Mr. and Mrs. Gerald Nevas, who were celebrating twenty-
five years of wedded bliss, according to notes Pomfret trans-
formed into:

"Now a madrigal for loyal Mr. Nevas, who for a quarter-
 century saw no need to seek pleasure, comfort or refuge in
 extramarital nooks, crannies or crevices,
Being perfectly content with Mrs. Nevas's."

"I hope for his sake he's drunk," Enid whispered in alarm.

Fortunately Mr. Nevas was, or close to it, judging from his
roar of laughter, and even Mrs. Nevas seemed delighted
behind the hands she clapped to her face.

But after rattling along for ten minutes or so in that risky
vein, Pomfret gave a charming finish for another middle-aged
couple, in this instance newlyweds. They were out with a
contingent from the United Nations being given local hospitality for the weekend. They both had posts with the U.N., he

as a secretary with the Italian delegation, she in some clerical capacity with the Greek. They had met there, in fact. His name was Ciccarelli, hers had been Taxipopoulus. After some syllabic fun with those, Pomfret wound up:

> *May multilingual Manhattan*
> *Afford the fulfillment they seek;*
> *If he shows her plenty of Latin,*
> *She may give him a little Greek."*

The comedian also acquitted himself satisfactorily, despite some familiar material such as an abrasive mother-in-law and the age of the magazines in his doctor's office, so that when the show was over a general feeling of buoyancy pervaded the old shed. Everyone at Jacquemoux's table was happy, most ordering dinner or a sandwich. Pomfret ate like a horse, justifying the name of the joint. A clubwoman stopped by to invite him to participate in a symposium on the subject of "The Identity Crisis in Contemporary Poetry." Jacquemoux liked what he'd heard and offered him an engagement of two or three weeks. He also said he'd put in a word for him with the owner of the Dull Roar in Chicago, who was a friend of his. Swirling hit it off with the Miller's Daughter, sitting beside her throughout dinner, and then dancing with her.

"What will you do after this?" he asked as he piloted her around the crowded floor. "Something else lined up?"

"Oh, I think I'd like to hole in somewheres and try to write a few songs. I've got half a dozen half finished. You know, folk songs" — she screwed her face up in an expression of extreme doubt and misgiving — "folk songs you write today all sound so — ersatz. You know? Not all wool, but fifty percent nylon and polyester. You know?"

"Oh, not yours."

She laughed, and her breath in his face made him think of warm peaches. It was getting hot in there, and her steaming fragrance excited him, as did the feel of her bare back on the palm of his hand and the steady tickle of her corn-silk hair against the back of it. Facts verified the legend that she could sit on her hair. The question was whether in a few more years she mightn't be able to stand on it. "I may make you listen to a few."

"Nothing would give me more pleasure."

"Actually I like this town. Avalon's become a suburban joke, but I like it. Could a girl get a couple of rooms here for a bit?"

"Well, that kind of rental is tough, but hey, my wife is subletting a small apartment she got stuck with. The friend she sublet it to wants to move out. I think there are a couple of months left on her year's lease."

"Isn't that your wife over there? She's dancing pretty cozy with Mr. Impromptu. Aren't you worried?"

"Oh, that's all right. He's her brother."

The quizzical look the Miller's Daughter returned at that, drawing her head back a little, made Swirling himself wonder what the devil he'd said. He maneuvered her around so as to get an unobstructed view of Becky and Pomfret, and indeed one would not, from their manner and the intimacy of their positions, have taken them for brother and sister. Which of course they weren't really, Swirling reminded himself, and told the Miller's Daughter, to his immediate vague regret. "They're not, duh, consanguineous," he said, and laughed. He hurried back to the previous subject. "Look, I'll look into that sublet if you'd like."

"Would you? And let me know. I'll be at the Walker Motel for a couple of weeks."

There was only the one show, and their party broke up a little after midnight, with the joint still jumping. The Swirlings rejoiced with Pomfret as they sped homeward, glowing as one with his success. Becky, sitting between the two men in the front seat while Swirling drove, twittered happily on about it, banging Pomfret's knee with his held hand as she recalled highlights of his "triumph." It was hardly that, in Swirling's view, but he would not begrudge praise for an extremely difficult accomplishment. The least one could say about an extemporaneous poet was what Dr. Johnson had about the woman preacher and a dog walking on its hind legs. Billing Pomfret as the only practitioner of that art in the country, or even the world, was probably no exaggeration.

But their euphoric mood was in for a rude jolt.

Just before fitting his key into the front lock, Swirling glanced in through a small windowpane in the door, and immediately realized that something was amiss in the house. From a light or two left on, he could see that a vestibule table had been knocked over and that a vase that had been standing on it lay shattered on the floor, its flowers strewn about in the resulting puddle. "Vandals," was his instantaneous thought. The others shared his suspicion when they had looked for themselves.

"There's that bunch of punks who call themselves the Sidewinders," Becky reminded them. "They vandalized a house in the next block — smashed mirrors, cut up pictures." Her voice had sunk to a whisper. "Should you go in, Bob? They may still be — Let's go see if the back door was broken into. This one hasn't."

Swirling thought a moment, then said, "No. They'd have heard us already, and that's the way they'd go out. We can't take a chance unarmed, at least with Becky."

"Let's go somewhere and call the cops first," Pomfret suggested. "These creeps when they're high on something. . ."

"Oh, to hell. I'm going in. You two wait out here till I let you know the coast is clear. If I frighten them out the back door, O.K."

His chief concern as he fitted the key in the lock was the Jawlensky. Becky's mention of slashed pictures had roused that fear, and he considered the coincidence of their having talked about the Jawlensky tonight a bad omen.

After opening the door, he entered as noisily as he could, preferring scaring off any burglars to playing the hero — certainly having no stomach for a confrontation with the Sidewinders, a band of hoods with revolutionary pretensions; hence the swath they had been cutting through privileged bourgeois suburbia, smashing up the contents of colonials and split-levels.

"Anybody here?" Swirling called. "Who the hell's in here, goddam it!"

He stirred up nothing but memories of Mrs. Tarbell similarly shouting up the stairs when showing the house, with himself the object of timorous inquiry.

He proceeded further. A disemboweled pillow next met his eye, its stuffing strewn about the floor from the foyer to the living room. A table lamp was knocked over there. He snapped on a light switch. He hardly dared look into the corner where the Jawlensky hung. He expected to see it slashed to ribbons. But it hung there still, unharmed. As he took stock of the room, about which were scattered some more eviscerated cushions, he heard a rustling noise behind him, and heavy breathing. He spun around, with a stab of icy fear.

He saw a pair of baggy, watery eyes, and a long pink tongue hanging out beneath them.

Mrs. Gluckstern was still looking for her tennis ball.

Eight

"I HAVE VERY LITTLE CHARACTER, but what there is is sterling."

That was what he now sometimes said and oftener secretly thought, in the one case facetiously, but in the second more or less seriously, hoping it might be so. Then what he possessed of solid worth might be likened to a fine but incomplete set of flatware; or to Katharine Hepburn's figure, of which Spencer Tracy remarks in *Pat and Mike*, "Not much meat on her, but what's there is cherce." He had for years remembered the observation as being made in the scene where Tracy is massaging her — another example of the curious mental tricks we play on ourselves. Because catching a television rerun of the film he saw that Tracy makes the famous assessment when turning to appraise the striding Hepburn out-of-doors.

What little quality he possessed, then, was cherce. That must be the limit set to any self-commendation. It was in the area of sexual relations that most of the silver was missing — or gold, to give him that — and introspection consequently most racked. His self-justification is summed up in the cry "Monogamy is just too goddam much to ask!" It is uttered as though from a cross on which convention is crucifying him, and from which he must simply be let down now and again for a bit on the side — to use one of Pomfret's more horrid Anglicisms. As with Becky when he was married to Enid, now with the Miller's Daughter when married to Becky.

That was the trouble in a nutshell. Unfit for either marriage or adultery, being restless in the one and remorseful in the other, Swirling often came to compare his plight to that of the platypus, that whimsically improbable little creature that is both aquatic and terrestrial and yet not comfortably either, and so an amphibian *manqué* into the bargain. It kills its water prey and then slinks off with it, stored in cheek pouches, to eat it on dry land, perhaps out of a sense of guilt over the element to which it has been disloyal — certainly out of insecurity of some sort. Its domiciling is equally muddled. The female cohabits in a burrow with her mate but only until it's time to have her young, precisely when one would think an adult male around the house would be welcome, at least a stabilizing factor. But no, off she waddles to lay her eggs in a separate burrow of her own building — leaving the male with still more on his conscience. Possibly he secretly thinks she does the work alone in order to make him feel a cad about *that,* a churlish reaction that only makes him feel it the more. To lay her eggs? Yes, for the platypus is, finally, further biologically scrambled in being an oviparous mammal. Abhorrence of the divorces that alone release our Swirling from the captivity under which he chafes supplies a similar last dimension to his confusion. A slightly duckbill nose may have started this whole chain of analogy in his mind. At any rate, it sharpens his identification with a curious beast that, though of the lowest in the scale of mammals, shares a distinctive trait with us, the ostensibly highest. The platypus yawns.

Swirling was waiting for an opportune moment to release a yawn that had been bottled up in him for a quarter of an hour, as he listened to the Miller's Daughter sing and play some of her own compositions, or rather the incomplete versions of songs she was working on. She sat on the floor, with the zither in her lap; Swirling in an easy chair, facing her. They were both naked. She sang experimental phrases and picked out trial chords, starting and stopping, repeating and changing. A large rhyming dictionary lay open on the floor beside her, which she kept consulting and paging back and forth in. The song she was working on was a ballad called "The Night I Wept in Chillicothe, Ohio." With a sad glissando on the zither she tried "the time we said goodbye-o," carefully watching Swirling's response, but immediately pulled a face, rejecting it herself.

"Pomfret's the one you should be asking advice from," he said. "He spits rhymes."

"Just comic ones. Not what this needs."

"Yes, well, I'd ditch the Ohio part, for a rhyme I mean. It's a trap. Oh me oh my-o. Heaved a tender sigh-o. Life's no slice of pie-o. Dump you into bathos every time, when what you want is pathos. I'd frankly get out from under Chillicothe too. That kills it aborning. It's one of those cities writers keep using because they're innately funny, like Perth Amboy and Kalamazoo."

"This rhyming dictionary is incredible," she said, riffling its pages against her thumb. "It's by Clement Wood. He was a poet himself." Her lowered head gave Swirling a chance to uncork his yawn, though he instantly felt another working its way up inside him, like an imp in a bottle. "Daddy says he could rig up an IBM machine to feed me any rhyme I wanted."

The Miller's Daughter's father was a computer expert, apparently in great demand as a programmer. Divorced, he lived alone in New York, where she was trying to get the three of them together for lunch sometime. An ominous sign.

The scene here was back again in Mrs. Pesky's garage apartment, which the friend to whom Becky had sublet it was now in turn passing along to the Miller's Daughter — whose name was Julia Griswold. Since Mrs. Pesky rented it furnished, everything about it was familiar to Swirling, especially the bird's-eye maple bed to which Julia now began to give unmistakable signs of wanting to return. Setting the book and zither on a table, she came over to the chair in which Swirling slumped like a man who had dropped into it after a hard day at the office. Lowering her head, she flung her hair forward over it and swept it slowly from side to side across his face and chest. In the course of one of its pendulum swings he glanced at a clock. Half-past nine. Becky would be home from a midevening French class at Back to School shortly after ten-thirty. He was supposedly at a kickoff dinner for a United Fund drive, and should be home not too much later than that, in order to avoid suspicion of the kind he and Becky had together generated in times past. He did his share of doorbell ringing for that and other worthy causes, but the boredom of kickoff banquets was something he felt justified in shunning. He did enough without listening to block captains urging the troops on to make this a banner year.

As Julia gave the rumpled bedsheets a cursory tidying, he put his head out the window to make sure his bike was still there, propped against the willow trunk much too thick to accommodate the chain he carried in the tool kit. On arrival for his trysts with the Miller's Daughter, he still hunkered down low as he shot past Mrs. Pesky's bay window, another familiar behavioral piece in the pattern. A philanderer is often a man in two ruts instead of one. Only the interruptive tread of Mrs. Pesky herself on the stair, on some mission legitimate or contrived, was needed to make the mosaic here complete.

Union being more prolonged this time, Swirling was able to provide the Miller's Daughter the slow, steady preparation she needed for the "deep orgasm" she never tired of distinguishing from the less profound "outside" one. Her eventual paroxysms were like an upheaval. The springs beneath them twanged like her zither going berserk, and the bed seemed to dance. Their crescendos tumultuously combined. Sexual rapture does obliterate the other senses to the extent quite justifying the French term *la mort douce*, literally enough in this case to say that it was only when Swirling had regained consciousness that he felt the burning strands of pain down his back and flanks inflected by Julia's fingernails in her own blind swoon. Later she sponged his welts with cotton and warm water, and as he lay on his stomach he warned himself to keep them from view at home, where such lacerations were not a standard connubial hallmark.

He didn't like to love and run — detested the term — but as Julia discoursed on the two kinds of orgasm, here he was watching the clock again, whose hands crept steadily toward the hour when he must be off.

"Men just have no sense of the difficulty sometimes involved for a lot of women, even those who can honestly be called high-sexed. And I'll tell you why. You're about to get a surprise. Ready?"

"Shoot."

"The human is the only species of which the female has orgasms."

"You're kidding."

"Not in the least. Men are always astounded when they learn that. But it's a fact. No wonder the mechanism is so hit-or-miss. That clitoris can't be much more than a million years old, or even if it's a few million that's still nothing in evolutionary time. It's a wonder it works as well as it does."

Swirling had often observed that people's gestures usually had nothing whatever to do with what they were saying. They served no pantomimic or other illustrative purpose. They were simply something to do with your hands, or possibly the motor discharges of nervous energy generated because you were talking to somebody. Becky plain flung or waved her hands about in all directions. Enid had a habit of crossing her hands at the wrists and then separating them at some word to be emphasized in a sentence, as though breaking an invisible thong. Leo Ludlow had a curious idiosyncrasy which consisted in holding one hand out perpendicularly in front of him, with the palm parallel to his body, and then moving it forward and backward as though slicing the space before him into segments. Many women repeatedly held a hand in a loose fist at their breast and then spread it open, flinging their fingers outward in your direction, before preparing the maneuver all over again. Now here was Julia twirling one index fingertip around the other, sometimes reversing it, as she discoursed on the intricacies of the female orgasm. Perhaps there was some subconscious belief that she was weaving an argument, and the fingers were like bobbins shuttling steadily on a pair of spindles.

"With you it's simple. Slam bam thank you ma'am."

"Oh, now, Julia, come on."

"I mean your sex in general, Robert dear. You yourself are a wiz at lovemaking. You know how to play tunes on a woman's body, with the most tender attention to zones. You know? You've discovered the pattern for me, the combination that opens my safe, and you follow it every time, but never mechanically. You have real virtuosity, such as I'd given up hoping to . . ."

Here the dissertation was less tedious than before, indeed

123

had begun to acquire marked cogency and interest, but it still smacked of the textbook — and another yawn was calling for release. Swirling could feel it there, crouched like a reptile on his diaphragm, certain to uncoil at any moment. He wanted to draw a pillow over his face long enough to get it over with, but Julia sat propped against the back of the bed on both of them.

"The distinction between the external and the internal orgasm is something men can't be expected to understand because there's no counterpart in their own makeup. In fact you're bored by the whole clitoral-vaginal thing, aren't you?"

"I wouldn't say that."

The plan for escape without being too obvious about it consisted in a variety of stratagems he had used with success before, to be executed with an illusion of leisure he had become quite skilled at conveying. He would climb out of bed straightforwardly and while articulating some response to what Julia was saying or had just said. He would carry his comment briskly forward as he made directly for his high-ball, in this case standing on the bureau. The appearance given, namely of having risen just to finish it off, would be sustained for a few moments while he flourished it in gestures as animated as his remarks. He was keeping the conversational ball rolling. But in doing so he would have been sidling imperceptibly toward the chair on which his coat and trousers were draped. Then still talking, or listening, he would dress, but dress abstractedly, as though not entirely aware that he was getting into his clothes at all. And before he knew it the thing would be done, and he would be shooting out of the driveway under the broad beam of light slanting from Mrs. Pesky's window, crouched over the handlebars like a six-day cyclist streaking for the finish line.

He was so late getting home that Becky was not only back from her French lesson but in bed and asleep. And with Pomfret in Chicago just then, with an engagement at the Dull

Roar, Swirling had an unexpected boon: the peace of the house to himself. He undressed quietly and without turning on the bedroom light, got into his pajamas, and stole down the hall to the extra bathroom he used for himself when there was no guest, for the nightly ritual he had come to think of as Facing the Caricaturist. Starting as an idle game, it had gradually taken on deeper meaning as an exercise in conscience, or punitive introspection, one that was, at this point in the history of his transgressions, not without certain self-flagellating features.

A mischievous spirit inhabited the medicine-chest mirror. It took the form of a crick in the glass running roughly in a diagonal from the lower left-hand corner to the upper right, zigzagging somewhat in the middle. It was this irregularity of which the Caricaturist made use in taking Swirling off with sometimes infernal cunning. The craftsman lurking, himself unseen, in the recesses of the medicine cabinet might be thought of belittlingly as "derivative," or respectfully as "versatile," depending on how you viewed the influences on which he successively drew. Swirling thought of him as a conscious parodist employing a variety of styles in order satirically to pillory his subject.

He had for some time been under the spell of Rowlandson, using the English draftsman's line and brushwork to mark a certain, oh, coarsening of Swirling's features, to emphasize to the subject his accelerating physical indulgences as middle age wore on. But lately reflections of Swirling's face in the glass had thrown off unmistakable hints that the Caricaturist had moved on to a new master, of greater urbanity to be sure, but making for more devilishly crafty effects. Yes, there could be no mistaking it: he had clearly edged into his Max Beerbohm period. Lampoons recently executed while the subject was shaving, and utilizing steam as a medium, left little doubt of that. That Swirling didn't like what he saw but drove himself to look might be taken as further proof of his own finely honed talent for self-torment. No matter. Tonight he spared himself nothing. Having kept his head lowered while he brushed his teeth, he at last, queasily, raised his eyes.

What he saw wrung a low cry of "No" from him even as he granted the validity of what he faced. This was the Caricaturist at his wickedest. The subject had tried to smile amiably for the artist, but the result had been but to invite exaggeration of a mouth recognized as sensual enough in all conscience — an opening on which the Caricaturist had quickly seized, while also amplifying a certain incipient jowliness. There was still an extra twist of the knife. He had used Swirling's features to execute a quick pastiche of Beerbohm's own caricature of Oscar Wilde. "No," Swirling said again, but there it was: the same sense of burbling ribaldry overspreading a face beaming a message of total self-gratification. In another twenty years, unless he mended his hedonistic ways, it would be the even more devastating Toulouse-Lautrec Wilde: the mouth by then a sort of moldy fig pursed between even grosser gills. All that could be fairly adumbrated now by a slight shift of his reflection to the right, where the crick in the glass was most pronounced. Why hadn't previous owners ever had it replaced? Maybe the bathroom had only been used by children, who liked its fun-house-mirror aspects.

What was the moral of Swirling's masochistic use of it? Should he turn over a new leaf, or go on as he was, wringing all he could out of life knowing that that was how he was going to wind up looking anyway, a seedy Lautrec relic? Life has no destination, except the old glue factory, so enjoy the ride. That sort of thing. The Nichevo bit. Soon enough he would be that old man in Byzantium reduced to soul clapping hands for every tatter in its mortal dress (had Yeats ever been more achingly ironic?); therefore remain "caught in that sensual music" for as long as you can. He would recant repentance, and rededicate himself to a life of any pleasure that didn't cause another pain. That was his morality in a nutshell, solemnly restated as he dropped his toothbrush into its slot. He would gather rosebuds while he might, bleed as he must from the thorns.

Now for the whiskey he had promised himself. He had once accidentally found the flavor of bourbon mingling with the aftertaste of toothpaste surprisingly delightful, like a kind of peppermint liqueur, and that was why he had his nightcap after brushing his teeth. He would probably have a second, and then maybe even a third. He wasn' in the least sleepy. What the hell. He would get a little drunk and do his exercises. He had been neglecting them of late, owing mostly to the tedium of enacting them sober — a tedium worse if possible than a kickoff dinner at the Y. Yet people seemed to like public dinners, and after-dinner speakers being reminded of stories and telling them to put their shoulder to the wheel and go over the top. Rum lot, people. Lucky there was no crick in the full-length mirror screwed to the back of the door of the bedroom he used for a dressing room, or the Caricaturist would really have socked it to him! He pounded his stomach with his fist as he stood before it now, at the same time contracting his middle. There seemed as much fat as muscle there. Yes, he would get a little stewed and do those bloody pushups.

He slipped downstairs and poured himself a generous slug of booze. After a sip or two he got down on the floor and did twenty pushups, the glass conveniently beside him on the carpet. After a short rest and another sip or two, he turned over and bicycled on his back. The little he pedaled about town in real life came nowhere near rating as "adequate exercise," according to his doctor. Still, he could take pride in not being slavishly reliant on automobiles, and thus seeing no need for a second car.

As he pumped somewhat tipsily away he worried about the

Beerbohm Wilde. It continued to nag; that is, the Caricaturist's fluky approximation of it did. To have done that particular job on Oscar, Max must have seen him laughing, and laughing like hell. It was at odds with the usual picture of the orchidaceous wit languidly dispensing prefabricated epigrams. Be that as it may, there was about him, Swirling, none of the hee-hawing self-dispersal caught in the famous cartoon. Was there now? And he was no fop. It had required Enid to tell him not to wear brown trousers with a blue jacket, Becky to edit the collar pins out of his button-down shirts. He was no help in selecting drapery and upholstery fabrics, and his taste in wallpapers likewise exempted him from suspicion in that area. And as for that male cow of Lautrec's crossing his mind, Jesus, that was simple association of ideas, was it not? No, he had nothing to fear from that famous psychoanalytic fix on your Don Juan: "Incessant sexual athleticism is the direct reverse of what it appears to be." Baloney. That was a bum rap as far as he was concerned. He wasn't Trying to Prove anything. He was just determined to enjoy himself as much and as long and as often as he could. He was, in plain English, cunt-crazy. He couldn't get enough of that ineffable commodity. It had taken a close brush with death (however imaginary) to make him realize it. Oh, he could imagine what a lifetime of womanizing would have him looking like at seventy-five or eighty: could even see how Lautrec might go to town on him. But it wouldn't be as the desiccated *flâneur* by a long chalk! Some sort of fleshpot clinker, sure, but not that. Swirling actually had a picture of himself in old age tucked away in a corner of a desk drawer, souvenir of a college class comedy in which he had played a village duffer, for which he had been expertly made up by a professional enlisted for the production by a drama coach with pull. Whenever in danger of mending his ways, of successfully fighting off the temptation embodied in some girl he'd met in a magazine office and half promised to call, he would get the photograph out and look at it — and run howling to the telephone, as Auden said the poet ran howling to his art. Or was it the writer? Well, he was neither, and that was another wound to clasp a naked woman to, like a poultice. Only the other afternoon he had decided against giving the Miller's Daughter a ring and gone to the beach instead to divert himself. There he had seen an old man shuffle across the sand and wade slowly into the water, using a walker, and had run to the nearest telephone.

Three nightcaps not only proved an aid to all this moral inventory, but had him feeling quite good into the bargain, so that he wandered out the kitchen door into the warm summer night and began chinning himself on the limb of a maple tree. Twenty was the goal he had set himself, but twelve was as far as he could get, this far along in his repertory. Sitting on the terrace, puffing, he wondered whether all this exercise was really good for you. Weren't there two schools of thought about that, the medical and the sybaritic? No, damn it, this was rationalization. The snugness of his pajama waist was reminder enough of what he must keep everlastingly at if he wished to retain the favor of girls in their twenties as he bowled along through his own forties. He would chin himself the other eight, after a rest, and then chuff a turn or two around the yard. He should jog more. But first just another finger or two at the bar. Jogging toward it, he stumbled against a hassock, and something about the chain of details made it occur to him that now might be a good time to polish up a little on his Groucho.

He really must work up a routine for the Heart Fund benefit, having copped out on Birth Defects, to say nothing of having welshed on his promise to Cerebral Palsy. Was he afraid he would come a cropper? A clown who has made himself a laughingstock is not a pretty thing.

"My wife and I have been hassling a lot lately," he suddenly began, resolutely snatching up a moldy cigar that had done months of service as a prop, "mostly over her family, but we're hoping for improved relations. If her mother loses about forty pounds and her brother gets a job, that'll be two improved right there. She's been putting all the household money in the market, some growth stock she says will triple in a month. 'I should clean up,' she said, and I said, 'You certainly should, just look at this place.'" He walked straight onto and over chairs as he prowled the room. He set one neatly over on its back by planting one foot on the seat cushion and the other on its top. "My first wife brought in a second income and even a third. She was a strip miner. She worked in the coal pits during the day and on the burlesque stage at night. A little gardening I do helps make ends meet. My strawberries are the envy of the neighborhood. 'What do you put on them?' somebody asked only today, 'Manure?' I said, 'No, just cream and sugar.'" He picked up a vase, a bit of chinoiserie of which he examined the underside. "Just as I thought — the Wrong Dynasty."

He righted the overturned chair and sank into it, breathing heavily. The room swam a little. He decided to light the stogie, but it turned out to be even fouler than expected, and he set it by after a few nauseated puffs. "El Ropo Smello-dora," he said. He felt pleasantly squiffy, and it was in that mood that he finally turned out the lights and went to bed, where he lay thinking about the Miller's Daughter and speculating about their next rendezvous.

That was the one that resulted in disaster.

He was supposedly taking an article, on the growing popularity of polo among young people, into a New York magazine office, but planned to use a local messenger service which made two deliveries from Avalon to the city per day, so he could spend a few hours with the Miller's Daughter. Making telephone connections with her from a public booth caused him to miss the morning run, so he went straight to her place, intending to leave in time to drop the manuscript off for the afternoon schedule. When he got there he realized that in all the fluster of conspiracy he had snatched up the wrong copy from his desk. It wasn't the finished version, but a previous draft. That meant he'd have to leave much earlier than he'd intended, so he could whip home again before dashing on to the office of the messenger service. They made home pickups, but that was of course out of the question. He might even have to take the article into New York himself. And even now he would have to cook up some story about having noticed his mistake on the train halfway into town.

The instant he opened the front door of his house he sensed something suspicious. There were voices upstairs, and a bedside radio going. Pomfret was back, and Becky could be heard laughing at something he had just said. *Petrushka* was coming over WQXR. Both it and the voices seemed almost certainly traceable to the guest bedroom. There was no doubt that a dalliance was in progress. It was unmistakable, even without one's clearly understanding what was being said. Swirling stood frozen with indecision. They had obviously not heard him come in. Should he make his presence known? Should he leave, having drawn all the conclusions he needed? What was audible only confirmed suspicions. Classic surprise would serve no purpose.

The copy he wanted lay on a desk in a small alcove off the living room which he used for a study. He stole over on tiptoe to get it, then back again, hoping to escape undetected. But as he regained the vestibule Becky was heard coming down the stairs, tying the cord of a bathrobe, as she called out something about checking a loaf of bread she had in the oven. Swirling could not light out the front door without being seen, as he'd have had to streak past the foot of the staircase she was descending. So on instinct he popped into the closet. He stood still as a mouse while the Miller's

Daughter had breasts like warm spumone and eyes the color of chicken broth.

All might yet have been well had not Mrs. Gluckstern entered the picture just then. She had waddled into the hall (her great dugs grazing the parquet, oh, *natürlich*) just as the intruder shot into hiding, pulling the door shut behind him. Either that aroused her curiosity or she thought some sort of game was being played with her, because she began sniffling and scrabbling at the door, trying to nudge it open, thus confirming Becky's suspicion that she had heard something. Her footsteps stopped at the foot of the stairs. A pause, then she could be heard slowly advancing across the hallway. Inch by inch the door opened.

Swirling stood as he had been standing in the closet upstairs, slightly stooped so as to avoid striking his head on the crosspole, and Becky's expression now was comparable to Enid's when the two of them had surprised *her,* in happier times. She even gave the same involuntary gasp of surprise. Swirling's face was in total disrepair. It was like something he was trying to gather up after it had fallen on the floor, like a china dish the fragments of which we stoop to sweep into a dustpan, prior to throwing them out.

"Well," Becky said, with an accusatory tone understandable enough in the circs, as it was Swirling who had been caught, and caught red-handed at that. He had been caught in the act of catching in the act lovers who were rendered, thereby, vastly less guilty than he himself, since his offense was the pettier, though theirs might be the graver. It had some scale to it, some scope. This was for the birds. Such, at least, must be Becky's grasp of this appalling tableau: a cuckolded husband upended in one of a number of closets in a house apparently built to accommodate such confrontations, or doomed by some curse to go on having them.

It was necessary for him to snatch the offensive immediately.

"So!" he said, marching out after flinging a coat sleeve out of his hair. "You two." But his hangdog expression, one of complete chagrin, betrayed the hopelessness of his cause, if that cause was the recovery of his grievance. No way. The wrongdoers had wrested that from him — or he had handed it to them on a silver platter. He took one last stab at regaining the *j'accuse.* "Incest."

"Oh, for God's sake, stop being melodramatic. So," Becky went on, fluidly resuming the offensive as though he had never babbled this Sophoclean folderol, "spying. On your wife. Sneaking in here like a —"

"That's not true. I came to —"

"Of all the —"

"— back for my manuscript. This one. I swear. Then when I realized you were — what was up — not that I hadn't suspected it — realized you were here and would know what I heard, well, I just thought I'd hide in here till I could get away. That would at least have spared us all this hideous embarrassment."

It was no use. Either Becky didn't believe him, or, what was more likely, she needed to believe in his paltry espionage, must, in order that her guilt be overshadowed by his.

"At least let's spare Pom. Something like this would shatter him."

"I suppose."

The mounting strains of *Petrushka,* together with some bathwater Pomfret had running, had prevented his hearing anything of the exchange below.

"Please go. *Please.*"

She seized Swirling by the arm and urged him toward the door, through which he ducked like a philanderer fleeing a home-returning husband. He leaped aboard his bicycle and pedaled off as fast as his feet could carry him.

Nine

AS OFTEN when feeling especially guilty about something, and what a heel he felt after taking his wife in adultery, Swirling went to see his father, paying off a bit of accumulated moral debt in that neglected quarter. The intervals between visits themselves gave him a bad conscience. It had been months now since he'd driven out to the New Jersey retirement home where the elder Swirling had lived practically since being widowed, seven years before. Maple Lodge was run by the church the Swirlings had always attended, except for the son whose baptism "didn't take," as relatives sadly joked about his descent into unbelief. The Lodge charged members of the denomination a mere twenty-five dollars a week, as against two hundred for nonmembers, for which Swirling thanked Almighty God, as it was he who footed the long-enduring bill.

Swirling had packed a hamper of goodies with which they were to picnic on a riverbank a few miles from the Lodge, but it was raining cats and dogs when they got there, so they had their picnic in the car. The hamper sat between them on the front seat, and a bottle of by now lukewarm rosé stood on the floor, secured between the old man's feet. They had not been munching their cold chicken and potato salad long when Mr. Swirling said:

"I don't have much longer to live."

Swirling had had his *déjà vu* as his father cleared his throat, preparatory to getting off what one knew was coming. Hadn't there been enough of that leitmotiv? Enough of *memento mori* with everybody in reasonable shape, at least for his age? There was nothing more wrong with his father than with himself or Becky. Discreet inquiries at Dr. Dundee's had revealed she had tricked him by dramatizing an anxiety no greater than most women carry with them through their adult lives. He had married her out of — no, not guilt, though God knew he was loaded to the scuppers with that cargo. He had done so in what he'd seen as a chivalric challenge to his manhood. He might be a rat, but he was no mouse. But *memento mori* would be the death of him yet — those and clothes closets between them bade fair to do him in.

"Why do you say that, Pa?"

"What's the use talking about it."

Swirling knew perfectly well that his father was slanting crabwise toward his usual insinuation: that Swirling should take him in "for what years remained to him." He would make the pitch in his own way at some unpredictable point in the afternoon. Swirling hadn't told him about his divorce from Enid, not alone to spare his old-fashioned feelings. He knew the old man would have pointed out like a shot that now his filial obligation could be discharged without prejudice to his marital; the excuse that "it wouldn't be fair to a wife to wish an in-law on her" would be liquidated. At least until he remarried. Then the specter of domiciling him with

Becky had raised its head. Picnicking there in the pouring rain, Swirling smiled at the thought of mixing those two in a common household. Then instantly had a brainstorm. It would be a capital device for scaring off the Miller's Daughter if she persisted in hints about marriage after the split-up for which he and Becky now seemed headed. Munching a deviled egg as the rain made a kettledrum of the car, he roughed out a general scenario. Single once again, or at least separated, he would have his father out for a week — as he and Enid had often done — and ask the Miller's Daughter to dinner a time or two, to meet the parent Swirling deemed his first obligation. It should drive all thoughts of marriage out of her flaxen head, to say nothing of Pa's scuttling gratefully back to Maple Lodge with the sound of zither music in his ears. Two birds with one stone. Swirling even enacted Becky's crafty little smile, screwing his puckered mouth to the left. No, it was to the right that she habitually twisted it.

Was he a bastard? He often wondered. Could not the amount of sheer self-flagellation over it be construed as qualifying the charge, even to the point of canceling it out? That would make it like the sin against the Holy Ghost as explained by his boyhood ministers in Kalamazoo. He could remember Reverend Ten Eyck in particular saying straight out from the pulpit, "If you worry you might have committed it, you haven't." Similarly, if you realize you're a fraud, you aren't. Did that wash? Again, he wished he knew.

"Of course you'll inherit all my patents."

Swirling often wondered whether the other inmates didn't think the man who talked about his inventions belonged in an institution of another kind. One was a hollow bar of soap designed to solve the problem of those last little scraps left over from an exhausted cake, always such a nuisance whether wastefully thrown away or frugally accumulated until there were enough to squash together into a reusable clump. Swirling was almost certain he remembered it as a

gag in a radio script years and years ago, but his father had
come by the notion seriously. And maybe it wasn't so
ridiculous at that. After all, there were now hollow ice cubes
mass marketed for bars and restaurants. Another idea was a
fork for eating spaghetti with a crank at the eater's end by
means of which the tines could be twirled around among the
noodles. That had been actually marketed as a gag, Swirling
having seen it in a novelty shop window. It was no use
arguing against his father's belief that the idea had been
stolen from him. But there was one of his inventions that
made sense. That was an appliance for electrically scouring
skillets and roasting pans and even bathtubs. Many a house-
holder scrubbing away with steel wool and elbow grease, to
say nothing of scullery toilers in restaurants, must have wondered why such a tool hadn't been perfected before. Yet no
kitchen-appliance manufacturer seemed to market one. Mr.
Swirling had experimented with all sorts of abrasive fabrics,
wrapping them around eggbeaters and potato mashers and
what-not in experimental tests, and now claimed to have
found an arrangement that worked, and to have "three or four
concerns interested." He had gone so far as to have registered a name for his invention: Power Skower. Who knew?
His ship might yet come in.

They helped themselves to seconds from the hamper,
heaping their paper plates with more potato salad and cole-
slaw, a forkful of which fell on Swirling's lap when his father
accidentally jogged his elbow. As he tidied himself, he had a
sudden sense that the pitch was coming. The old man often
got in his points with cunning obliquity — in fact he reminded Swirling of Becky. This time he led up to the
subject with a new ploy. He slyly needled his son with "The
Blue Room," not the chorus but the verse part, which he
began to hum and then sing, as though absently, looking out
the window on his side and pausing once to take a sip of the
tepid Tavel from his paper cup.

"There's your mother's room, there's your father's room," he sang. He had the lyrics wrong, having altered them to suit his propaganda, whether consciously or not. "There's your mother's room, there's your brother's room" was the Hart rhyme. Not that it mattered. The point was the same. Indeed, the authentic version of the cozy hospitality prevailing in that unbelievable love nest of yesteryear was even more relevant to Swirling's case, though that was unsuspected by Pa, who, after singing the measures pertinent to his cause, launched his customary exegesis of the lines.

"*Both* in-laws they've got living with them, each with his own room at that. Fat chance you'd hear of any such thing in this day and age when nobody copes and everybody ignores his God-given obligation. At least I'll go to my grave knowing I had a three-generation household, one of the last it seems like. I'm sure you remember Grandma living with us when you were a little tyke. Your mother's mother, not mine, but no matter, we were all good to her. Including you, far as that goes. I can see you now, fanning her with a magazine on those hot summer days we could get in old Kazoo. But now we want nothing more to do with old people," he ground remorselessly on, "thereby distinguishing ourselves from the American Indians, Orientals, Africans, and other primitive societies." This last burst offered an example of the fine phrases he would pick up from magazine articles and television panel discussions on his pet subjects, and store up for later polemical use of his own. Like many another oldster complaining of failing memory, he managed to remember what he wanted. "The fifth commandment is the only one with a promise attached to it. 'Honor thy father and thy mother, that thy days may be long upon the land which the Lord thy God giveth thee.' I'll say no more."

Swirling was filling up with guilt like a litter bin with refuse. He had tasted enough incrimination for one day — or week. What he needed now was a little justification. He sought it by acting on a secret hunch that his father was a lot happier at Maple Lodge than he let on, and that the displays of melancholy could be taken as partly an act aimed at melting a son's heart. To test his theory, Swirling stuck around for a bit after bidding his father goodbye that evening, in order to observe him on the sly among his fellow tenants. He stayed through the afternoon, took him to dinner in town, and then dropped him off at Maple Lodge with the promise to telephone him very soon. Watching from the car, he saw his father hurry inside so as not to be late for a parlor get-together scheduled for eight o'clock. The rain had stopped and, spying through a window from the lawn, Swirling saw a changed man. He was the life of the party. He led the assembled group in a songfest, starting off with "Hail, hail, the gang's all here, mustn't say the naughty word, mustn't say the naughty word, mustn't say the naughty word *now!*"

They all applauded themselves, and then in a buoyant mood consulted mimeographed sheets for the words of the next song. Mr. Swirling sawed the air with both arms as he conducted them in the old rigmarole:

How much did Ioway, boys, how much did Ioway?
She weighed a Washington, boys, she weighed a Washington.

What did Delaware, boys, what did Delaware?
She wore a New Jersey, boys, she wore a New Jersey . . .

Swirling hurried back to the car, while from within came the fading strains of "What did Tennessee, boys, what did Tennessee?" He was halfway home before he doped out the answer to that one. Of course. "She saw what Arkansas, boys, she saw what Arkansas," he sang at the top of his voice.

The familiar satisfaction of an obligation once more discharged was as palpable as a good taste in the mouth, one that, however, gradually changed to another which he recognized for what it was: the brackish reluctance to return home. How could he ever explain to his poor old church-elder father what they all were there, now, in the notorious suburbs: the Bohemian bourgeoisie.

Standing outside in the yard a moment, after locking the garage door, he could hear that Pomfret was at the piano, up to one of his musical didoes. One was to render classics in a manner hardly envisaged by the composer. He would thump out Chopin's Waltz in C-sharp Minor, or one of the more delicate nocturnes, with a vehemence usually reserved for the *1812 Overture*, keeping the loud pedal down throughout and flailing the keyboard with all his might. He said he did this to clean out his liver, and those of his hearers too, as well as to purge the selection itself of accumulated platitude. Or he would play the "Ride of the Valkyries" with a gentle touch, leaning back with his eyes closed and dreamily negotiating the Wagnerian bombast with a lingering, feathery nuance. Or he would reverse tempi. He liked to see how long he could string out "Flight of the Bumblebee," and claimed to have given the "Minute Waltz" a reading of a quarter of an hour. Tonight with especial relish he was knocking out putrid "Liebestraum" with "Anvil Chorus" hammerblows and at breakneck speed. Only in this way, he maintained, could you clobber the treacle out of it.

He also liked to garble famous literary pomposities. "As Emerson said, a shadow is but the lengthened man of one institution." "Goethe's statement that music is melted architecture . . ." "You're all familiar with Boswell's remark that Dr. Johnson liked to walk on all fours, but seldom did it well." There were also some weird tastes in food. He enjoyed slicing bananas into clam chowder, and was at least once seen spreading pâté on vanilla wafers. But he had suffered. He had suffered. In college years he was a perennial victim of pranks by those of denser sensibilities, having once been seized and blindfolded by a dozen classmates all of whom called each other Joe, and forced to repeat a hundred times, "Them sheeps ain't his'n," a sentence every word of which was wrong, as expiation for his pernickety English.

"How was your father?" Becky asked, looking up from her needlepoint.

"Fine."

She had never met him. He had never met her mother. Christ, what was the country coming to?

Then it was time for the Eleven O'Clock Wrap-up. Becky smiled with anticipation as Pomfret seized a banana from a bowl of fruit for use as a mike.

"Flash. Agrohusbandman Robert Swirling, of this city, has after thirty years developed what livestock farmers have hoped for since the beginning of recorded time, namely a strain of cows with legs three inches shorter on one side than the other, for grazing on hillsides. Reached for comment at his home on Benson Road, Swirling said, 'I believe it's a major breakthrough. Cattle stumbling about on grade pasture — there is about them anyway a certain, shall I say, bovinity — cattle bumbling about on declivities has produced many unfortunate effects, not the least of them curdled milk, which in turn has resulted in cheeses rarely, if ever, stormproof.' Active in community affairs, Swirling is also a carburetor buff, boasting the largest collection of carburetors in the country ... Another fatality in the mounting epidemic of housewives bored to death in the suburbs ..."

"Play us a little Scriabin, Pomfret, do. I feel in the mood for Scriabin tonight." Swirling rose with his highball and, parting the draperies, glanced out at the moon. "The hour between eleven o'clock and midnight is the ideal one for those bleeding nuances."

But calculated asininity is a very tricky art, and if he kept this up they would very quickly recognize a caricature of Pomfret, poor or otherwise. But madness, murder or suicide,

141

whichever came first, drove him on to giving the screw another quarter-turn.

"It's the hour when these sudden hungers seize us, the need for an emotional snack, like raiding the aesthetic icebox, don't you know. Tonight I could positively wolf Scriabin. Not any of the sonatas, but, oh yes, by all means the 'Two Dances,' the exquisite 'Guirlandes' (how much more expressive a word than 'garland' — the word itself *hurts*) and then the all too brief 'Flammes Sombres,' with its sense of languid delirium, the liquid sonorities of those discreetly writhing rhythms, clairvoyant of fevers to come no doubt, but without the programmatic sweat of the tone poems . . ."

The others looked at him as if he had gone off his chump. Had he been drinking before this? No, they didn't get it. That this was a whole nother crock of sauerkraut altogether that he was opening. He would have to graduate the schtick, or spell it out plain: that nothing he was babbling could be put past the copywriters for those LP album envelopes, on which he liked to gorge himself. He was in fact giving them actual Scriabin sleeve-copy rant that he had personally come across. He stepped over to the record cabinet and read them a little direct, to point up the sort of thing he was trying to do. He was "being" an album pocket. But it had been a close shave, diverting himself off the Pomfret lampoon in the nick of time. That would have torn it! That would have put them in a pool of blood around here.

In any case, the scenario had changed. Swirling would not go berserk as originally planned, running amok among the draperies on the cue word from Pomfret, such as "shedule," or a heartily accented "good show," and then gutting Pomfret by shoving the nozzle of the vacuum cleaner down his throat. No, that was out. He was going bonkers in a manner at once more subtle and comprehensive. His choice of request just now had been made with that in mind. He had secreted in the piano a bomb wired to go off when the famous "mystic

142

chord" of Scriabin's was struck, a chord existing nowhere else in musical literature to Swirling's knowledge. This chromatic hallmark of the Russian's was an arrangement in fourths by which Scriabin had hauled the musical carcass to the threshold of atonality, across which Schoenberg then dodecaphonically dragged it. Whether there would be enough left of this triple ménage to bother dragging *out* over the threshold after the explosion would be hard to say. In any case, the chord, at least as Swirling understood it, appeared among the aching harmonics of "Flammes Sombres," which Pomfret was now successfully coaxed into playing.

Swirling having already wired the explosive inside the piano, this would seem, then, Die Nacht, or It. Two hands exactly placed upon the black and white keys, and uh-fuh-dee, uh-fuh-dee, uh that's all folks. Swirling's choice of the "Flammes" for detonation constituted an especially satanic twist. Mmbahaha!

Pomfret sat down, rubbed his hands, and began. Swirling settled down with his highball — his last, of course. Becky was swinging gently to and fro on the swing as the opening passages filled the room with their tonal perfume, wincing harmonics reminiscent, even at such a radically far remove, of the Russian's first god, Chopin. The influence was clearly there — that incense for the ear. The fatal chord drew near, a chord of such racking near-atonality that it must in the chromosomic beginnings of Time itself have been wired by the Almighty for the preordained, apocalyptic moment that would blow them all to kingdom come. Swirling would thus be a mere instrument of the divine will. The running amok bit was out because according to the basic premise in the new scenario he had already cracked; or more accurately *been* cracked, delicately, a poor egg spoon-tapped by the Omnipotent for some inscrutable purpose. And the plan was providential, merciful. It was better this way. For now no longer would they have to bear the burden of themselves and one another. For Swirling himself the end would be a release. No longer would he have to turn himself steadily on the lathe of compunction. No longer wince at the thought of his betrayals. No longer wince at the thought of so wanting his brother-in-law out of the house that he had toyed with the idea of driving him out by inviting his father for a stay, which made him wince anew at *that*. And then wince reflexively at having winced . . . Oh, it was too much!

The chord was almost here, a mere measure or two away, now. Swirling's heart began to pound. Sweat beaded his brow, his hands grew clammy. His mouth was dry as cork. Perhaps he should stop the performance before it was too late. He half rose out of his chair, aware that Becky had stopped swinging and was watching him with an odd expression. The moment was here — this was the chord. Pomfret raised his arms, hunching his shoulders, then brought his hands down on the appointed keys.

The soft pedal mechanism of a grand piano is a shift device which moves the entire keyboard to the right. Either the composer called for a pianissimo here, or, more likely in such a climax, the performer elected dramatically to mute one moment of it. In any case, the intricate wiring inside the piano did not take soft-pedaling into account, and so the moment passed without incident.

Pomfret finished, and they both applauded. Then he played the "Guirlandes," and after that a couple of other short pieces. Then Swirling said he was tired, excused himself, and went to bed.

Ten

"I KNOW YOU DON'T SAY GRACE ANYMORE, haven't for years, but do you ever pray at all?" Mr. Swirling asked his son.

"No."

"Why not?"

"Because nobody's listening."

The old man was cleaning up in the kitchen after dinner, using the latest makeshift version of his Power Skower on a pan in which a roast beef had been cooked. The abrasive with which he was experimenting in this mock-up was a metallic scrubbing cloth tightly wrapped around the twin propellers of an old potato masher, which revolved in opposite directions. The shaft of one of them got jammed in the chuck into which it fitted, and he swore mildly in Dutch till he got the mechanism going again.

Pomfret was on a tour booked for him through an agent he had acquired. Becky was with him, after an agreement with Swirling on a no-fault divorce action as the most decent means of dissolving a union admittedly beyond repair. No-fault seemed fairest as they were both to blame. The Miller's Daughter was also once again on the road, singing at the moment in Kansas City, and Swirling had moved into Mrs. Pesky's garage apartment the day after she vacated it. She had been conclusively discouraged by Swirling's announcement that his father would presently join the scene. Swirling himself regarded the stay as only a visit, but the return to Maple Lodge was put off time after time while the old man tried to wangle an appointment to demonstrate his invention for something called Modern Kitchens, Inc., a firm with offices in nearby suburban Chesterwood.

"The other day you used the expression 'act of God,'" he reminded his son, continuing the discussion.

"Ironically. I was referring to that church that was demolished in a cyclone the day after it was dedicated."

"Ach, ja." The old man chewed his tongue as he worked on the gadget.

The visit originally intended for a week or so became two weeks, then a month, as he persisted in his siege of Modern Kitchens by telephone and letter. An appointment did seem imminent. Meanwhile, they passed the time by arguing religion and related subjects.

"It was a shock to me to learn you've had not only one divorce but are getting another." They were having after-dinner coffee in the tiny living room, one haunted, for Swirling, with the ghost of more than one inamorata. "But I know times change, and who is any one of us to criticize another. As Jimmy Carter emphasized again the other day, we shouldn't judge that we be not judged."

Swirling grinned engagingly across the room at his father.

"The author of that charge spent most of his life coming down on people with both feet. Judge was practically all he did. He gave the Scribes and Pharisees bejesus till the very words are terms of opprobrium. He called people liars, hypocrites, whited sepulchers, every name you could imagine. He was a grade-A vilifier. He drove the money changers out of the temple with a whip he made himself. He snubbed his mother and upstaged his family. He finally judged God himself. 'Why hast thou forsaken me?' And it wasn't just people who got his flak. He even cursed that poor little fig tree. He was not a very nice man, but then he probably came by it honestly. His father is said to have driven the first couple out of the garden for nothing more than picking fruit he himself hung on another tree by way of temptation. So it ran in the family. But I mean why should we worship in a deity behavior we wouldn't stand for for two minutes in a next-door neighbor? Adam and Eve were kicked out of paradise in what Cyril Connolly called a fit of womanish spite."

"That that friend of yours who teaches at Ypsilanti?"

Swirling substituted fact for tribal lore. He hung the earth in space and time, a mote spun out of a delirium of gas and dust five billion years ago. He elucidated Christianity as a hodgepodge of pagan mythologies — the religions it had to swallow up like a conglomerate to stay in business. Missionaries gave heathen gods Christian names and then reported that a wholesale conversion had taken place.

"How do you know the earth is five billion years old?" his father asked.

"Scientists can measure lead deposits left in rocks by the decay of radioactive materials. The more lead isotopes the older the rocks. It puts the earth's crust at about two billion years. The earth was molten a few billion before that."

"How do they know how long it takes the lead to form?"

"I don't know. Some kind of atomic calculation I suppose. You take some things on faith."

"Ah ha!"

"Look, Pa. When science predicts an eclipse you go out confidently and watch for it. When you have an infection you take the streptomycin science invented. When it puts a man on the moon you stand in awe. So why not trust it, and related disciplines, when it shows us that our religion is a conglomeration of fairy tales?"

"What are some of these pagan religions we whipped Christianity up out of? I'm only asking. We haven't had a discussion like this in a long time. What are some of these gods we took over?"

"Oh, I don't know. In the first place Christianity is a rehash of the cult of Mithra, the Persian sun god we worship every Sunday and whose birthday we celebrate every December twenty-fifth, whether we realize it or not. The date for Christmas was deliberately fixed to wipe out opposition from that deity, whose miraculous birth, incidentally, was witnessed by shepherds, and whose devotees had baptism as well as a sacramental meal of bread and wine. The Egyptian version of his sun festival was celebrated on January sixth, so let's steal their thunder by scheduling something known as Epiphany then. Easter myths about the resurrection of a mangled god have of course celebrated the rebirth of vegetation for thousands of years with hundreds of deities. Christianity also ripped off the Eleusinian mysteries of the Greeks, in whose version Hades was the death god to whose underworld you were banished for eating forbidden fruit." Swirling swept on in what was itself a miraculous reconstruction of a long-ago sophomore term paper on comparative religion, flooding back with remarkable clarity. "The Eleusinian mysteries took nine days — remind you of anything, like the novena? — and there was also holy water, wouldn't you know it. The Christian images of the Madonna and Child are obviously a rerun of Isis suckling her son. The statue of the good shepherd carrying his lost sheep and the pastoral themes on Christian sarcophagi were also taken over from pagan craftsmanship, and let's see, what else? Oh. The Romans I believe it was, or maybe the Greeks, had a god who walked on the water, and of course we took Pan for adoption and raised him to be a devil . . ."

But at last the appointment with the Modern Kitchens people came through, for eleven o'clock on Friday morning. Swirling drove his father out to Chesterwood, halfway between Avalon and New York. The old man carried the Power Skower mock-up together with a can of Ajax scouring powder in a carton on his lap, cradling his brainchild, and in the back seat was a rattling jumble of greasy and otherwise dirty roasting pans, kettles and skillets, the unwashed accumulation of a week's dinners with which he would conduct the demonstration.

"You actually going to take all those filthy things into this man's office?"

"How else can I give my demonstration? Ask Mr. McKay to bring some from his house? He's a high-muckety-muck, vice-president in charge of development they call it, so he'll have the key to the executive washroom. Or probably a bar in his office, for entertaining clients. It'll have a sink."

Swirling saw his father, dressed in the pants of one suit and the coat of another, both pinstripe, penetrating a battery of crisp receptionists and other supernumeraries through a sequence of offices with yellow leather divans, carrying a heap of unwashed utensils and a reincarnated kitchen gadget.

They drove along in silence for some time. Then Mr. Swirling said:

"Wasn't there a philosopher or something, a Frenchman I think, who said that if you're in doubt about whether there's a God and an afterlife and all, why, just go ahead and believe? It's like a throw of the dice. If it's all true, you're saved. If it's all bunk, what have you lost?"

"That was Pascal."

"So what do you think of that line of argument?"

"I would say that if I were God I'd have a very low opinion of that kind of mealymouthed pussyfooting your way into

149

heaven, or trying to. Because I wouldn't let anybody like that in, and I rather think Jesus would give him short shrift too. Make a scourge of cords and send the little weasel back to Tuscaloosa."

"I see what you mean. And I suppose you're right — about the whole thing, I mean. You've been hammering away at it since high-school days. Now suddenly you've set me to thinking. Never too late to learn."

He began humming "The Blue Room."

The corporation offices looked like a country club. A long, low-lying building of concrete and glass nestled among needle and broadleaf evergreens, invisible from the road and approached by an eighth of a mile of winding gravel driveway. Old Swirling ran up the front steps to announce himself. He looked small and pathetic as he vanished through the doors, the old man from Kalamazoo swallowed up by all that glazed chic. Waiting, Swirling glanced over his shoulder at the pile of stuff in the back seat, and shook his head. He could even smell it, the cold lamb fat providing the dominant note. The whole venture seemed preposterous, Modern Kitchens included. They were all engulfed in absurdity. All that would be needed to cap the grotesquerie would be for the old codger to succeed.

He reappeared inside of two minutes, with instructions to drive around to the back of the building where there was an entrance to the company cafeteria. That was where the demonstration was to be conducted. Swirling helped him carry the stuff in, and then waited outside, as his father wished. He strolled around the grounds for half an hour or more. The gravel on the driveway looked as though it was taken in every night and washed, preparatory to being strewn about again the next morning. He felt almost guilty soiling it with his shoes.

At last his father emerged, flushed with excitement. The pans loaded on his arms were spick-and-span now. The three executives present at the demonstration had all been impressed. The invention they wanted to keep for further study, and consideration at higher levels.

"I think they're definitely interested," Mr. Swirling said, as off they drove for home again.

They had dinner out, and a brandy afterward in the little parlor. Swirling grew drowsy in his armchair. A nap might be a good idea, as he hoped to sit up and catch a late showing of *The Bank Dick* on television. Dimly, he heard his father say:

"Well, you've convinced me."

Swirling came to with a bob of his head.

"Convinced you?"

"About religion and all. How it's an illusion. You marshal your arguments very well. No wonder you were the star debater at Kalamazoo High. You were always fair though, admitting many people need these illusions to lull themselves through life. 'It's a great life if you don't waken,' you used to say. You always put things so well."

Swirling grunted modestly, giving a little shrug. Then he dropped off again.

"Sooo, I've decided the only thing for me to do — intellectually honest thing I mean — is to resign from the church. Tender my resignation."

Swirling mumbled something else noncommittal. Then he came to as though galvanized by an electric charge.

"What!" he said, horror-struck. "Are you mad? Do you realize what that means? What you're saying? You can't get the members' rate at Maple Lodge any longer. You won't be able to go back there. Are you forgetting what nonmembers pay? Two hundred dollars a week. Which is a hundred and seventy-five dollars more than" — he didn't shy at the facts — "than I have to cough up now as it is. I haven't got that kind of money." He was wide-awake now. "So you get that nonsense right out of your head, do you hear? There *is* a God, Voltaire that great mocker himself said, 'I see a clock, I assume there's a clockmaker.' Now you stop this foolishness. We with our finite minds —"

"It would be hypocritical, taking their reduction under false pretenses. When I can no longer subscribe to their doctrines. You've shown me the light."

"Doctrine schmoctrine! You've been a loyal churchgoer all your life, supported it with your hard-earned money week after week. You're entitled to the" — he was going to say "discount" but substituted a less crass-sounding word — "benefits available to you in your sunset years. I think it's ridiculous of you anyway to let every Tom, Dick and Harry talk you in and out of one thing and another."

The elder shrugged sympathetically. "What can I do? I've got to be honest."

"You leave that to me. And I'm saying honestly that I can't afford two hundred dollars a week or anything like it. It'll send me to the cleaner's."

His nerves were jangled. He'd slept poorly the night before, and dreamt among other things that his penis had turned into a cactus bristling with needles, so that no woman could ever again receive him. He'd had, in the dream, the clearest sense that the development had been punitive. That was it, for him. Quoth the raven. Uh-fuh-dee, uh-fuh-dee, uh that's all folks!

The thought crossed his mind, against all the reason supposedly enthroned there, that this turn of events, too, could be construed as divine retribution. Heaven forbid! How much better to be marinated and cooked in the Catholic rather than the Calvinist conscience. Every week to have the sludge cleaned out of your transmission in a latticed booth. "Father, I am insatiable. I eat, drink and sleep women. They are my downsitting and mine uprising. I have yet to meet one I didn't want to stoke. I have stoked my wife's best friends and her worst enemies. Like the Fellini hero of 8½" — here the face behind the wicket became knowingly Italian — "I cannot pass anything up. Since I was here last time I've slept with another. Two!" "Ten Hail Marys." "Better make it twenty." "Why, my son?" "I've got a nooner lined up with a girl at the office."

Twenty Hail Marys and the thing is done. But as a Calvinist, that Puritan doubled in spades, that unexorcisable Pauline bluenosed scourge of the flesh, as a Calvinist with your catechism not only in your brains and your guts but in your very balls, the guilt is unresolvable. The check is never paid. Nothing on account will stop the dun on your conscience. Somebody else must foot the bill. Of course somebody else had — that was the atonement in which the Catholics also believed, but somehow they could see it as all marked paid and forget about it and enjoy themselves. Or so it seemed to Swirling.

He was more than wide-awake now. A suspicion dawned on him. He rose and stood over his father's chair, fixing him with a steady eye.

"Is this just a ploy on your part? To get to stay with me? Now I'll have to keep you?"

"Oh, by the way, what's a ploy? I've been meaning to ask you that. New word that keeps popping up."

"You know very well what I mean. A stratagem to gain the upper hand over somebody. Never mind whistling 'The Blue Room' again. We've had quite enough of that. You've pulled some fast ones in your time. Not for nothing did they used to call you Foxy Bob, and you're getting foxier every year. But this is too much."

His father gave him a wounded look, finished off his schnapps, and went to draw his nightly bath.

Listening to the water drum into the tub, Swirling had an idea. Maybe even an inspiration. Mrs. Pesky. Why not enlist her in his cause? The problem would be just her meat, from what he'd managed to gather about her on short acquaintance. She was devoutly religious, a convert who had become evangelical herself. She had a "Honk if you love Jesus" sticker on the bumper of her car. The car that had been instrumental in her meeting his father. It had got stalled in the driveway one day, and he'd got it started again. He'd not only pointed out that her carburetor was in need of repairs, but had fixed it himself. That had led to their taking tea together a few times in her parlor. The two seemed to hit it off. Yes, Swirling could do worse than try to recruit her to his cause. She might just help get him past the dilemma that now threatened to confront him: keep his father permanently, or sink hopelessly into debt. Never able to marry, much less live with a woman, or even take one to his place for the night. His style was already cramped in that regard. A life of poverty, chastity and obedience loomed like a specter before him. He might as well enter a monastery.

He stepped to the window and looked across the yard at Mrs. Pesky's house. It was all lit up. He could see her chubby figure moving about in the kitchen. He put on his coat, called to his father splashing about in the tub that he was going out for a breath of air, descended the stairs down which he had so often scuttled to avoid Mrs. Pesky's inquiring eye, and knocked on her door.

"Do you have a moment?" he asked when she answered it.

"Sure, come in."

She was having some after-dinner coffee, in which he joined her at the kitchen table. After a moment or two of shilly-shallying, he came to the point.

"Mrs. Pesky, I want to talk to you about something. It's my father."

"A fine man. I like him."

"And he does you. But I'm afraid now he's got into a mixed-up state. He's been led astray by — well, never mind

154

that part. You're a good and sensible woman. Deeply religious. That's the main thing."

"'Only an armour bearer, proudly I stand, waiting to follow at the King's command,'" she softly sang.

"That's the thing. Mrs. Pesky, I sorely fear that at this most inopportune time in his life he's losing his faith."

"Doubts, eh? How so?"

"Oh, influences brought to bear on him. One in particular —"

"Some smart aleck spouting atheistic talk, eh?"

"Something like that."

"Knows more than God. I'd like a few minutes with that gazebo."

"I thought you might help straighten him out. My father I mean. Get him off the" — he saw no need to mince words — "broad highway to damnation and back on the straight and narrow."

"That's a tall order. Have you talked to him?"

"A blue streak. Labored with him, in the old phrase they used in our church. Doesn't do a bit of good. He's going through a phase." Swirling took a gulp of his coffee and set the cup down again thoughtfully. "It's more than that. He's gone into some sort of tailspin, as people often do when they reach a certain time of life, though we know it could just as well be middle age or adolescence. You know — things boil up."

"*And* over," Mrs. Pesky emphatically agreed. "I know that from direct personal experience. I was knocked galley-west when my husband died. Saw no point. Then I heard this evangelist I believe I told you about. That was when I made my decision. It's so simple. You accept Christ and —" She snapped her fingers. "And the burden of your heart rolls away."

"Ah, yes, that old hymn. I remember it well. 'At the cross, at the cross, where I first saw the light,'" Swirling softly sang.

155

Mrs. Pesky joined him, lilting her head to the beat, and together they lifted their voices in a verse or two of it. Then she regarded him narrowly.

"What's your opinion in all this? Are you saved?"

"Not *saved* exactly —"

"You know what's what. You've been brought up in the fear and nurture. As President Carter said the other day on television, 'You must be born again.' You must have a spiritual rebirth. You've never made a decision?"

"I figured there was no need to. I was baptized into the faith, you see."

Here Swirling realized he was skating on very thin ice. Very thin ice indeed. He must plan with extreme delicacy to avoid the one most obvious pitfall to this ticklish project, namely, that his father might in the course of conversation with Mrs. Pesky reveal the culprit responsible for the apostasy, and along with it possibly the subverter's motive for now wanting his influence reversed. He must anticipate that by a deftly inserted word or two, and right here.

"The fact is, I've had doubts myself, but an open mind, I think. I'm, well . . ." He need not grope for the cliché. Mrs. Pesky had it ready, on the tip of her own tongue.

"You're an intellectual with something missing in his life."

"That's it! That's it exactly. You've put your finger right on it. Let's see, where were we?"

"You had these doubts."

"Yes. Well, it was in honestly airing them to my father that I may have contributed just a weeny bit to his backsliding. Now, my plan is this," he hurried on, "that you get him to go hear this revivalist you told us about, who converted you. You spoke of him only a few weeks ago. Is he still in Bridgeport? This spellbinder who if he's all you say he is may put my father back on the right track?"

"Wally Walker I would stack up against Billy Graham, and backsliders are his meat."

"Oh, wonderful."

"That's what revival meetings are for, the meaning of the term — to *revive* our faith."

"Amen!"

"Sure, I'll be more than willing to ask him along to the Tabernacle. I go every Wednesday. Maybe you'd like to come too."

"Of course."

"It's a date then. Who knows, you may be saved."

"I hope so," Swirling said.

Bridgeport wasn't far from Avalon, but getting to the Parkway and then from it and across town to the Tabernacle would take time, Mrs. Pesky warned, so they left nearly an hour before the revival meeting was scheduled to start, which was 8:00 P.M. Swirling drove them all out in his newly acquired secondhand Chevrolet sedan. Mrs. Pesky and his father sat in the back seat. Swirling did his best to keep the talk off the subject of religion for the duration of the ride through a light drizzle, out of fear of being compromised in Mrs. Pesky's estimation by something his father might let slip, or say outright, about his talking out of both sides of his mouth in this whole episode. Steering both the car and the conversation became a tricky business, as the traffic was heavy and his father insisted on airing his newfound perspective on Christianity as nothing more than a conglomerate that had got and stayed in business by swallowing up the competition.

"Did you know it's a hodgepodge of heathen myths?" he asked, and in the rearview mirror Swirling could see him gesturing knowledgeably as he addressed this poser to Mrs. Pesky, who was tightening her lavender gloves by folding her hands stiffly and squeezing the fingers down. "Fact. There was this Egyptian sun god — where we get our Sunday — a Greek or Roman deity who walked on the water,

157

another whose birth was witnessed by shepherds and who had a ceremonial last supper, and I don't know what all."

"I don't see what that has to do with it, on balance, you know," Swirling said over his shoulder. "That could be looked on as all part of the divine plan — preparatory elements, or rehearsals, so to speak, for the great climactic drama of the Incarnation. Don't you agree, Mrs. Pesky?"

"Yes. The forerunner principle."

"Ah, very neatly put. All sort of John the Baptists."

"And the pagan deities were just myths — nobody *saw* them —"

"While the historicity of Christ has never been questioned."

"They were preliminaries to the main bout."

"Love it."

"Who was it they claimed walked on the water, though?"

"Oh, Poseidon or somebody," Swirling said dismissingly. "Or maybe just commanded the water."

"They only *said* he did. Christ actually did."

"Way to go." Swirling had had a couple of drinks to oil himself for the ordeal, which he increasingly saw as necessary to save himself from insolvency, and to be justified on that ground. His father spoke up again.

"But Bob, here, claimed —"

"Have to watch this exit, or we'll miss it. Isn't this it, Mrs. Pesky?"

"Yes. And after we're off the ramp I'll tell you how to get to Park Street."

"O.K. No, it's all a question of how you look at this whole thing, whether an encrustation of myth invalidates a central truth, or value. Toynbee has a brilliant slant on it, incidentally."

"That that new superintendent of schools?"

"No, no, this is Arnold Toynbee, the historian philosopher. He has a superb passage toward the end of his *Study of*

History — I must read it to you when we get home, Pa — but his idea in a nutshell is that all other religions are partial by comparison with Christianity, because the saviors claiming godhead throughout the ages all lack the final and unimpeachable credentials — save one. There have been since the dawn of civilization hosts upon hosts, in varying degrees ranging from human heroes upward through demigods themselves. All of those fade under our scrutiny, and only the gods remain for evaluation. But one by one these too fall away, till only a single figure soars above the flood of contenders, to fill the whole horizon — the one savior whose claims to divinity have been validated on the cross. He alone has delivered the goods . . ."

Throughout this recapitulation, prolonged in order to stall for time, Swirling caught uneasy glimpses of his father waiting for an opening, which he now appeared to have, unless this was to become a full-dress sermon in itself.

"But only the other day you said —"

"I've reached the age when the cops all look young. You know that experience? Well, I must say that a lot of them also seem pretty fat. Look at that one across the street there. Just look at him."

"Well, it's sedentary work," Mrs. Pesky said. "Standing around all day twiddling a stick. Honk!"

"What?"

"At that driver up ahead."

"Got you."

Swirling had thought she had in mind his maneuver to pass the motorist, but now realized she was referring to the "Honk if you love Jesus" sticker on his rear bumper, so Swirling gave a blast on his horn as he shot by, receiving a prolonged one in return, which wailed in diminuendo behind them. The number of such stickers increased as they neared the Tabernacle, especially in the parking lot into which the faithful were already pouring in a steady stream, so that in the swelling honkfest in which Swirling joined he felt like one of a flock of geese forgathering in the ecstasy of the autumn weather.

The excitement continued to accelerate inside the Tabernacle, where an overflow crowd listened to a roaring evangelist of the old school deliver the kind of harangue that is to oratory as military marches are to music. Wally Walker was a large man with a shock of yellow hair that made him even more imposing. He sawed the air and he flailed it. He fanned it with the Bible he held in his hand when he had not thumped it down on the pulpit to emphasize something. He pointed upward to heaven and downward to hell. There was no question of observing the theater principle of "not starting too high." He started at fever pitch and worked up to delirium. For his text he had chosen some verses from the second chapter of Revelation. "He that overcometh, and keepeth my works unto the end, to him will I give power over the nations . . . And I will give him the morning star." It was to that promise that he really warmed.

"Do you want a star for yourself, to rule in glory, beloved? Pick one out. Would you like Aldebaran? Take it. Betelgeuse? Yours for the asking. Capella? Reserve it for yourself. There's mine up there, brethren, the one I've got dibs on. She's a beauty!" Then he shifted his syntax to accommodate an apostrophe to the celestial body itself. "I can look up at Rigel, that bright double star in the constellation of Orion, and say, 'I'm gonna boss you one day, from my mansion on Hallelujah Avenue!' And the same privilege will be yours, my friends, if you take the Lord tonight!"

Here the individual "Amens" from the audience that had punctuated his words from time to time swelled to a chorus. Swirling was thrilled in spite of himself. It was irresistible, the sort of vulgarity in which one should periodically wallow. It restored the tissues, it irrigated the arid brain. One was carried helplessly along as the evangelist lashed himself to a peak of frenzy.

"Do you want to reserve that star for yourself right this minute? Do you?"

"Yes!" came the thunderous response.

"Would you like to put in a call to heaven for it?"

"Yes! Amen, yes!"

"Then pick up the phone and do it, and do you know something else, beloved? You don't even have to pay! You can reverse the charges! Yes, sir, you can make that call collect, because the bill for that direct line to God Almighty in heaven itself has been footed by Jesus Christ for all time!" Here he actually executed a pantomime of reaching for a telephone and putting it to his ear. "Hello, Central? Get me heaven, and put me through to Jesus, and Operator? I want to reverse the charges. This is a collect call. I don't have a dime. I'm a poor sinner. So make it collect, and person-to-person!" The chills ran up and down Swirling's spine. The evangelist stepped to the edge of the platform and fixed his audience in a dramatic stare. "Won't you put in that call tonight? Right now! Come forward while we sing the hymn that tells you how to take advantage of this unlimited offer. 'There is a fountain filled with blood, drawn from Immanuel's veins. And sinners plunged beneath that flood lose all their guilty stains.' Hymn number 312 in your books. And after we sing it let's come forward, those who accept Him for the first time tonight and those who already have but want to renew that declaration. To take a booster shot of salvation. So act now! Sing all!"

Their party sat in the middle of a row to the right of the center aisle, into which worshipers now moved from everywhere in the auditorium as an organ pealed out a thunderous accompaniment to the hymn. Their pew soon began to empty, and Mrs. Pesky, who was nearest the aisle, rose also. Swirling got to his feet and motioned for his father to do the same, but his father seemed confused about what to do. "We're Mrs. Pesky's guests," he whispered in his ear. "Come on!" He grasped his father by the shoulder and shoved him bodily into the aisle, now thronged with the redeemed. Among other motivations, creditable or not, Swirling was suddenly swept with the realization that a secondary aim in his general scheme was to enhance his father's eligibility as a prospect for Mrs. Pesky's hand in marriage. Was he coming unwrapped? Probably so. But no matter. He shuffled into the aisle himself and then slowly forward to the altar, hymnal in hand, singing with the multitude.

Those making an initial decision remained, as converts, at the front of the church, to be received into the faith; those simply redeclaring their existing belief wound back to their seats. Swirling with the rest of his party made the circuit with the latter. Shortage of space necessitated the arrangement. Reverend Walker welcomed the newcomers into the fold, and then when the entire congregation were back in their seats, they sang a last hymn suited to the occasion:

> There were ninety-and-nine that safely lay
> In the shelter of the fold,
> But one was out in the hills away
> Far off from the gates of gold.

Then the benediction was delivered, and the revival meeting was over. Swirling felt exhausted rather than revived, and his father seemed emotionally wrung too: neither with his background of staid and even dour religious services had ever heard anything like it. The three got silently back into their car, and it wasn't until they were well along on the Parkway again that Mrs. Pesky asked what they'd thought of it. Swirling contented himself with saying that Wally Walker was everything he'd been cracked up to be. She wisely refrained from probing Mr. Swirling as to whether his backsliding had been checked, or even possibly reversed. He was visibly sobered by the evening's experience — which they topped off with a cup of hot chocolate in Mrs. Pesky's parlor.

Two other developments made for an eventful month.

Mr. McKay telephoned to say that Modern Kitchens, Inc. were prepared to offer Mr. Swirling fifty thousand dollars outright for the rights to Power Skower, and that mostly for the name, as they already had patents on two or three features of the mechanism that would have enabled them legally to go ahead manufacturing such a product without provable infringement on his own. He accepted the proposition. And two weeks later he announced that he was going to marry Mrs. Pesky.

Swirling went out and gave thanks at the nearest saloon.

Eleven

ANY SUCH HAPPY RESOLUTION of Swirling's own affairs seemed as remote as ever, if not more so. He now had to smuggle his women past both Mrs. Pesky *and* his father, when there was any such contraband to smuggle at all. His father moved into the main house while Swirling stayed on alone in the garage apartment on a month-to-month basis, not pressed to take a lease, thank God. His professional fortunes were at as low an ebb as his amorous just then, the demand for his articles having markedly fallen off, so he sometimes had difficulty scraping up the rent money, to say nothing of the installments on his used car. He continued to think of his new stepmother as Mrs. Pesky despite all evidence to the contrary. He tried to avoid situations in which he had to call her anything directly until he could hit on some satisfactory mode of address. The very thought of "Mother" or "Mom" palsied his tongue. Once, to get her attention, he had resorted to "Hey." He figured that when the moment struck

164

when a direct vocative was absolutely no longer avoidable, her first name might be managed. That was Cornelia. It would take a lot out of him.

His father was now his landlord, jointly with Mrs. Pesky, and because he depended on their good graces when he was a little short the first of the month, he wanted especially not to risk outraging their moral principles, which were particularly stern in matters of sex. (He had given up trying to explain to liberated friends the fell clutch of oppressive childhood pasts. He had a recurring dream, sometimes of nightmare scale, that he was back in Kalamazoo and trying desperately to hurry home on half-paralyzed legs in order to give account of where he'd been and what he'd been up to. He knew perfectly well that Mrs. Pesky had been from the start a stand-in for his mother, the surrogate scourge of his conscience; and that he was deceiving his mother when he cheated on his wife. All that.)

His garage apartment was not so much his castle that he didn't still shoot past Mrs. Pesky's bay window when he had contraband with him, the contraband under orders to keep out of sight by ducking her head or sliding down in the car seat as they went by. The problem of smuggling them in, for the night and especially weekends, became acute when, presently, Swirling found himself in up to his ears with a black girl.

He had read a review of a Jawlensky exhibition running in New York and gone to see it. It was a cloudy day, threatening rain, and as he walked from Grand Central to the Kobrand Gallery on upper Madison Avenue he carried a furled umbrella, occasionally giving it a propellerlike whirl by its malacca handle, the better to fancy himself a London connoisseur and collector out stalking the current art scene. Woolgathering aside, he was in point of sober fact out to see how much he was worth. He had gathered from the review by the *Times* critic that Jawlensky's star had risen steadily since his death in 1941, and while he was nowhere near abreast of Klee and the rest of the Blue Four, his position among the Munich pre–World War I avant-garde was established beyond question. So the wedding present the giver had admitted accepting from a hard-up friend in payment for a hundred-dollar debt was now worth — what? Five thousand? Maybe even ten, dared he hope? He was hard up himself now, and his heart was beating fast when he walked into the Kobrand Gallery.

He was the only visitor there, and as he strolled from picture to picture, pausing before each, he was struck by the expatriate Russian's powerful sense and use of color, the cumulative effect of which his own single possession had scarcely prepared him for. The critic had spoken of "demonic saturations of hot color" and "lyrical evocations of nature achieved by purely chromatic means" till hell wouldn't have it. Bold simplifications of contour verging on caricature in the portraits were reminiscent of Rouault, but there was something ferociously Slavic that also revealed the influence of Bavarian folk art. The brilliance of these juxtaposed reds and yellows and blues indicated to Swirling that his picture was probably in need of cleaning; he and Enid had sorely neglected as well as underestimated it. Neither had ever been very high on the pioneering Expressionists.

There was a young woman sitting behind a desk, and between brief machine-gun bursts of her typewriter Swirling felt her eyes following him as he circled the room, the idly dangled umbrella still doubling as a walking stick for a London blade communicating with every gesture and pose a casual sense of knowing his onions. A man appeared from a back room through a curtained doorway, and huddled with her in a whispered consultation over a sheet of paper in his hand. Leaving it on her desk, he straightened and likewise took Swirling in. He was short and bald, with a mustache so sharply waxed that it seemed the tips must prick him if carelessly fingered. Swirling stood before a portrait of a woman, leaning on his umbrella, one foot crossed negligently over the other. He suspected the watchers might suppose themselves to be penetrating somebody's imposture. They must be taught a lesson.

"Are any of these for sale?"

"Yes. That one you're looking at is. Those with red stars are of course already purchased."

"Yes, of course. How much are you asking for this one?"

"A hundred and ten thousand."

The parquet underfoot was also waxed, and the ferrule of the umbrella skated a good two feet across it, upsetting Swirling's balance and very nearly spilling him to the floor. The recovery of his aplomb was not the first order of business, but he managed to ask with some nonchalance, "Do you have a price list I might see?"

"Certainly," the man said, handing over a leaflet. "Are you interested in Jawlensky?"

"Oh, yes. I have one, marfact."

"Oh? Is it a portrait or one of the still lifes?"

"It's a still life."

Swirling studied the list, stroking his own mustache. The prices ranged from thirty thousand for some of the smaller canvases clear on up to a hundred and twenty thousand, though that was for the "Seasons" suite, the four landscapes that had elicited the critic's comments about lyrical evocations achieved through purely chromatic means. Purchased singly, the pieces would be forty thousand dollars apiece. Swirling stood absorbed before them, contemplating each in turn.

"I like the 'Spring' particularly. I don't know that I could quite swing a hundred and twenty thousand dollars at the moment, and it would be a pity to break the series up. I do covet the portrait of the woman too. Well, let me think about it."

"There's a Jawlensky in the Museum of Modern Art show I like. A charcoal drawing of a woman. Have you seen it?"

"I was planning to nip on over."

"When was your still life done?" Kobrand — it must be he — had a little the manner of a police detective trying to break a suspect's story down by interrogation. "Do you know the exact date?"

"Around 1912, I think. It's about the size of this one."

"It should be very valuable now," Kobrand said with a smile, "if it's genuine. Have you had it authenticated?"

A cold fear struck Swirling, like ice water running down his spine. What if it was a fake?

"It's, oh, fruit, and a vase, and beyond them a moon visible through a window. Vague suggestion of an animal in the distance. Like a goat." He had always thought the nocturnal background landscape reminiscent of Krazy Kat, but didn't say so now. Mr. Kobrand was shaking his head.

"What you think is a window sash is probably the frame of a picture. Jawlensky sometimes painted a picture against another painting. Like that one there."

"It came originally out of —" God, he hoped he was remembering the name correctly. "The Jerome . . ." he faltered, his memory of what he'd been told failing him.

"Oh, yes, the Arthur Jerome Eddy Collection in Chicago. That would probably make it genuine. He probably picked it up for peanuts. They are forging Jawlenskys like mad now. I had a fake in only yesterday. Man was outraged when I had to tell him. What's it painted on?"

"Cardboard," Swirling said, and watched the other with naked hunger.

The man nodded. "Sounds right. Bring it in. You may want

168

to raise your insurance evaluation on it, his prices have been going up so. It's probably worth, oh, fifty or sixty thousand if it's genuine, would be my guess. But don't take it to Parke Bernet. They charge. I'll appraise it for nothing, because I like to see them all. I handle only the German Expressionists, but *all* the German Expressionists."

"Oh, thank you. I certainly shall. And meanwhile let me think about the lady." He bobbed the handle of the umbrella lightly in the direction of the portrait. "Good day," he said, and sailed on out.

Swirling floated on a cushion of air down Madison Avenue, across town to Fifth and along Fifty-third Street into the Museum of Modern Art, hardly remembering that in a sudden downpour he had opened the umbrella only to have a gust of wind turn it inside out, so violently that he'd had to discard it in a trash bin. He paused in the foyer to mop his face and shake out his wet suit.

He readily found the Jawlensky charcoal sketch, admired it a moment, then continued his stroll through the exhibition, which was entitled "Twentieth Century Masters." Then as if in a dream — yes, that again, only ecstatically this time — he was toying with some salmon salad in the restaurant and gazing out the window into the dripping garden, at the Maillol, Moore and Renoir sculpture, the overpowering Rodin Balzac. Presently he became aware of a young woman sitting alone at a nearby table. She was the color of lightly creamed coffee, slim, with a face tapering perfectly to a small but firm chin, tilted almond eyes, and an Afro halo of restrained proportions. She was eating the same thing he was, or rather not doing so.

"You don't seem to like yours any better than I do mine," he said, an opening hardly up to standard for a Belgravian boulevardier on whose every purchase the art world hung.

She gave him a smile faint to the point of intimidation. He thought of Pomfret. What was that mot of his at the French restaurant, instantly seen as reversible? Oh, yes. He cleared his throat.

"The food in museums is about on a par with the murals in restaurants."

Again she smiled wanly, rather a feat with that dazzling octave of teeth.

"Have you seen the exhibit?" he asked.

"Which one?"

" 'Twentieth Century Masters.' "

"Yes. I see them all. I work here. I'm on my lunch hour."

"Oh? Where do you work?"

"Front. Print and book salesroom."

"Oh? Tell me, do you have anything on Jawlensky?"

"Of course. There's a book there, and some repros. You interested in him?"

He shrugged modestly. "I have a few. I knew that charcoal was in the show, so I thought I'd pop on over and have a gander at it." Ass! Yet he was powerless to stop this, turn himself off. The tide of intoxication swept him onward, toward success or a rebuff he wouldn't have given a damn about. He might strike out, but there was no harm in giving desire its head — the young woman was ravishing. He heard himself say, "Are you free for dinner tonight?"

"I don't quite know yet."

"When will you know?"

"After about five more minutes of this free trial offer." At last she laughed frankly and openly, and it was like a light being turned on in the room.

"I was hoping we might rip a chop. I have a pressing engagement," he Grouchoed it, "with that tailor down in the men's room at Grand Central. After he gets this suit back in shape I'll be ready for the evening. We can try for a play or a concert, or just sit upon the ground and tell sad stories of the death of kings."

"Yeah, I'm free. And may God have mercy on my soul."

Eight hours later, they faced each other across the last of a bottle of claret in a restaurant he'd made sure honored his credit card, while she told him in the nicest and friendliest possible way what a fraud he was.

"A *genuine* fraud, that's the difference. You yourself are genuine, a bit of all right, in this British-blade act you put on, or are today. You're O.K. underneath, with this — what's that word that begins with a 'p' that means a surface effect? Like on furniture."

"Patina?"

"Yes. This surface thing. I mean anybody can tell by looking at you you're — I mean your face is a map of Germany or maybe Holland —"

"Come on, you're cheating. You know it's a Dutch name, corruption of Zwerling. And patina's the *real* thing, the surface sheen that comes on something with age. I'm afraid the word you wanted was 'veneer.'"

"I had a roommate at Bennington who was Dutch, and she called it a cheese face. You're a nice big ball of Edam posing as a bit of Stilton with port. So never mind with the popping over and nipping on round and ripping chops together."

"You can give a chap rather a pasting on short notice."

"That's what I mean! You just did it again." She pointed a finger at him, finished her wine, and collapsed back in her chair with a burst of laughter. He supposed she'd had a little more than her share of the Latour. Not that it mattered. There was little or no malice in it all. That came — or something seriously resembling it did — when the subject of race relations came up. She was militantly eager to talk about them.

"We'd all be a lot better off if we'd just admit that prejudice does exist, and then try to rub along as best we can. Now wait. Don't try to tell me that deep down in your heart of hearts, where the masks are off, you can take me just as another human being. That you don't think of me as black, first and foremost and always."

"You're a beautiful young woman to me —"

"A sepia sizzler."

"Oh, Christ, let me speak for myself."

"You want to go to bed with me, not just man to woman, but because I'm black, and you've never had those hacks, or if you had, that was the kicks and you'd like to have them again. I can see you carrying me to bed like in those junky ads for those miscegenation movies, that junky copy that goes with the salt-and-pepper tableau, 'He holds in his arms the image of elemental woman.' That's you — may I call you Robert?"

"You've called me everything else. But my friends call me Biff," he said, for some reason fetching up from memory the nickname he'd briefly had in high-school days.

"And I'm Pauline, remember? 'Holds in his arms the *alluring* image of elemental woman.' I forgot that. Sure, I'll go to bed with you, Biff. But somewhere along the line that worm'll come out of the woodwork. I'll be black, you'll be white. You'll cop out. No matter how unprejudiced you think you are, you'll cop out. If and when the chips are ever down."

He had to scribble the tip on the bill to get out with enough to pay his parking check so he could drive home. Pauline Winchester lived with two other girls, and so they had to call it a night. She gave him her phone number, and the assurance that she'd go home with him the following Friday, which was three days off, and stay the night.

But Swirling sold two articles in rapid succession, and was able to afford hotel rooms in New York. Two months later he was short of funds again, and was faced with suspending their trysts or taking Pauline into the garage apartment. Infatuation won the day, or the night rather. It was toward the end of winter, therefore dark when he whisked her past the bay window on Friday evenings, and not yet light the next morning when he shot out of the driveway and back to New York and the Museum of Modern Art, where she worked three Saturdays out of four. It was on the fourth, when a fellow employee spelled her, that the trouble came.

They didn't wake up till half-past nine, or get up till after eleven. By noon they had breakfasted, and Pauline was poring over a railroad timetable in preparation for the trip back, which this time she would make by train. Swirling was adding their dishes to a mountain already piled up in the sink when he thought he heard a footfall on the outside stairs. He stepped over to a window and looked out. It was Mrs. Pesky, toiling upward with a mince pie she had promised to bake for him.

"Oh, my God, here comes my mother."

"How old are you?" Pauline asked mildly, over the schedule.

He glanced wildly around, feeling like a cornered animal looking for a place to hide.

"Go into the bedroom. Hurry!"

"Why? Let me handle this." She was wearing a mischievous smile, one not far from a triumphant smirk. It was the expression of someone with something up her sleeve. "You go in there. It'll be all right. You'll see. I'm dressed and everything."

"What will you do?"

"You'll see — Whitey."

She bundled him into the bedroom, where behind a half-closed door he helplessly listened to the ensuing dialogue. Through a crack in the door he could see Pauline snatch up a broom. She presumably held it in one hand while she opened the porch door with the other.

"Hello, I've got this —"

Mrs. Pesky's bugging eyes could be all too clearly imagined.

"You must be Mrs. Swirling."

"Yes."

"Biff told me a lot about you."

"Biff?"

"Mr. Swirling say dat what y'all call him. Ah'm Praline? Ah comes in on Saddies?"

"Oh. Oh, yes, I see. Yes, where is he?"

"Yo' son done gone into town. He be rot back. You done brung dat cher pah fo'm? Mmm, smell good. Mm *mm*."

"But his car is here."

"Dat what he done went about — get a mechanic. De battery daid? It need jumpin'?"

"Why didn't he take his bike?"

"Dat done broke too. You know what dey say, dem philosophers, 'bout de total depravity of inanimate objects? Yas'm."

Clutching his head in both hands, Swirling rocked it from side to side, as though miming, "Oy, oy, oy!"

"Yes, well, I promised to bake him a mince pie when next I made one for his father and me. I'll just put it on the kitchen table." Double footsteps as the devil followed Mrs. Pesky into the kitchen, where a gasp signified that the latter had laid eyes on the sink.

"Dat what Ah said when Ah see dat cher mess."

"I'll just leave the pie here. You from Norwalk?"

"Yas'm." Good God! He must put a stop to this travesty, step out, declare himself. But his feet seemed embedded in solid concrete.

"How did you get here, by bus? I don't believe I've ever —"

"No'm. Ma mama done brung me. She pick me up again at fo'."

174

"How much do you get, Praline? I've lost my cleaning woman. Course I only have work a day every two weeks."

"Ah jenny gets thirty dollars a day. It done jest gone up from twenty-five. Yas'm."

There were a few more footsteps, of indeterminate direction or purpose. As though Mrs. Pesky was hesitating about something. *Go*, Swirling thought. Then with horror he heard her say:

"Oh. While I'm here I must take a look at that bedroom ceiling. There's been a wet spot flaking away there and — What did you say we called him?"

"Biff."

"He said it's been getting worse. If it is, I'll have to have a roofer give me a figure."

"Ah don't see nuffin' wrong wit' de one y'already got, Mrs. Swirling. Dat a joke. Well, Ah'll jest get to work in de kitchen. Sho' needs it."

As Mrs. Pesky advanced toward the bedroom, Swirling's brain spun helplessly. He darted toward the bathroom, stopped, thinking better of it. Then he shot on tiptoe across the room to the closet. He pulled the door shut just as Mrs. Pesky walked in.

They stood not six feet apart, Swirling scarcely daring to breathe as he wondered what she might be taking in after more than enough time had elapsed for her to assess the damage to the ceiling. He tried to think what might still be lying about, on the floor, the unmade bed, or draped over a chair, that might betray double occupancy, as the hotels called it, and also reveal the malicious parody of which they were both alike the butt. At least they would have that in common! A pair of stockings? Slippers? Where was Pauline's valise? Her coat fortunately hung beside him here in the closet. Another closet! Would they never end? Would the woman never go away? If, suspicious, she poked her nose

175

into the bathroom that should tear it. A jar of cold cream, some mascara, a compact? But she left without looking.

"Yes, that roof definitely leaks," she said. "More expense. Any house can be a headache, but two! Don't ever be a landlord."

"Ah don't 'spect Ah ever will."

"Well, tell Bob I stopped, and have a piece of that pie yourself for your lunch, you hear? I pride myself on my pies."

When she had gone and Swirling had emerged, it was to find Pauline sprawled in an easy chair, roaring with laughter.

"I was right, you see? You see what I mean? When it came to a showdown, you copped out. Whitey."

"Now, wait a minute. *You* did this. You rigged it, to prove your point. Which *wasn't* the real point at all, from my point of view. I didn't want her to know I had a woman here — any woman. A female per se. Period."

"That's hypocrisy."

"You're damn great at telling people what they're like."

"All right, how would you have played it? If I hadn't jumped in?"

"What?"

"How would you have played it?"

Swirling looked around the room, as though the answer might be found in some corner of it, or lurking behind the furniture.

"I don't know. Just winged it, but how do I know how? Just introduced you as my friend and let her make what she wanted of it, or think what she wanted."

"So why didn't you? You let me get you off the hook the way I did, and damn glad you are that I did, now. Squeaked you out of your parents' finding out you're shacked up with a black girl."

"That's not the issue I tell you! Goddam you, you have no

idea how straitlaced these people are about sex. Sex qua sex. It's still thou shalt not commit adultery to them."

"But aren't you independent enough to let them know you want to lead your own life? Why pussyfoot?"

"Because I don't want to outrage their sensibilities needlessly! I don't like hassles. I can't stand hassles — including this one! Oh, what's the use? You've got the wrong end of the stick. We're talking about two different things."

Pauline sprang to her feet as he dropped into a chair.

"All right, let's talk about them one at a time. I'll grant you your end of the stick. If I was white you wouldn't want them to find me here either. That's that. But don't tell me it wouldn't have been twice as hard, ten times, a hundred times, with me. Admit it, and why. That's been my point all along, that deep down every white man has a prejudice, which he instinctively feels no matter what he says. Including liberals like you. You make a noise like tolerance but you don't mean it. There's a giveaway sting in that very word itself, because it means you're tolerating somebody, which is pretty goddam intolerable to us to begin with. Oh, it's fine when it's a Cause. Out there. When it's majority black rule for Rhodesia, way out chonder, and civil rights in Mississippi here. But when it strikes any closer to home than that, it's no go. You're a hypocrite."

"All right, I'm a hypocrite. But at least a couple of pathetic old people aren't walking around over there tearing their hair out. *I'm* doing that. And when there's nothing left of mine maybe I'll start on yours. You little bitch," he said, and laughed despite himself.

She struck a pose in front of him, her hands on her hips, her loins thrust forward, for all the world like a temptress in those movie ads she ridiculed.

"Let's lay it on the line. Would you marry me?"

"Oh, my God. You argue like a wife," Swirling answered

wearily. "The world is full of white girls I don't want to marry either. Do you want to marry me?"

"Hell, no!"

They both laughed at that. She knelt, parting his knees as she wriggled in between his legs. "You're stuck with me till four o'clock, you know."

He held her off by her shoulders, contemplating her from a distance as though he was farsighted, returning her arch smile with one of his own. "Whose wounds are you trying to rub salt into, mine or your own?"

"You don't have any wounds."

"Oh, no? That wasn't a rubber hatchet you were just playing with, baby. Oh, well. Shall we put the kettle on?"

Twelve

SWIRLING'S LIFE, seen as an odyssey of self-justification, like yours and mine, had reached a critical point. He *was* a fraud, a phony, a lecher and, as Pauline had said, a hypocrite. All this painful self-inventory moved him to seize an opportunity he saw as enabling him to make some kind of amends for a life of admitted self-indulgence and moral poverty. Happily in the circumstances, the challenge posed itself as a chance to strike a blow for the black cause.

One evening he ran into Enid and Leo at a party he was attending as an extra man paired off with a young woman who was studying for the Episcopal priesthood. Enid told him she and Leo were going abroad for four months and were looking for somebody to occupy their house in their absence. "Do you know anybody?"

"Yes. Me."

"Are you serious?"

"Sure. I'll go bonkers if I have to stay in that garage apartment any longer. How much are you asking — dear?"

"Oh, nothing. We couldn't get renters for that period anyway. House sitters don't pay. But look, it's not *our* old place on Chestnut Street. We're not living there anymore. It's more than we really need, and we can frankly use the rent from it. A whopping nine hundred a month. So we've moved into the place on Benson Road. You know, with all that wonderful closet space? Would it have memories too painful for you?"

"What wouldn't? Done and done. But tell me, did you ever have that fun-house mirror replaced in the extra bathroom? The one with the crick in the glass?"

"No."

So that was the first thing he did after moving, alone, into the house. His clothes hung up in the guest room, his shirts laid away in the bureau vacated for him, he went to face the Caricaturist.

There was never for a second any doubt of the phase into which the Caricaturist had moved since his work had been last seen. He was in his George Grosz period. The rest had been spoofs of varying amiability. This was Judgment Day. Swirling was offered back to himself as one of the artist's gallery of bourgeois profligates, each more sensual than the last — and not one sensuous! — lampoons of carnal self-indulgence so scathing as to seem almost a pun on the artist's name. "You've become a Grosz creature." He said it aloud. And it would be worse, the trend was irreversible. There would be eyes like those of predatory fish, heads like inverted brandy snifters, faces bloated with bestiality amid figures writhing in a hell of guilt. And he would be one of them. Ecce Homo! Derivative the Caricaturist certainly again was, but there was fiendish cunning in the way he caught not only the subject's sins but also the self-flogging instinct to seek out these successive portrayals. Yet there was one thing at which he balked, one detail he singled out as unfair. The curl to the lip, marked when the face was held just so in the mirror's irregularity, seemingly denoted greed.

He objected sharply, in one of the imaginary exchanges with the artist over the finished product.

"I'm not avaricious."

"Then why didn't you tell Enid about the Jawlensky?"

"It slipped my mind."

"You've seen her three times since your first visit to the gallery, and twice since you had the painting authenticated. The way you sweated that out! Beads of perspiration on your brow as Mr. Kobrand with a razor blade deftly cut away the paper on the back of the picture, read 'Stilleben, 1912' there, turned it over again and examined once more the brushwork before pronouncing it undeniably genuine, and worth in the neighborhood of sixty thousand dollars. Don't you think Enid's half-equity should be restored to her?"

"I've tried that over and over. She won't take it. We split our possessions down the middle, clean, fair and square, each turning his back on the other's half. Of course I'll offer her half of it again, if I sell it, but she won't . . . And she has property of her own. I let her have the house for God's sake!"

"It was hers in the first place."

No, he had enough to be forgiven without any imputation of guilt in the Jawlensky business, and when he saw a chance to go to bat for the Negro cause locally, and in so doing wage a struggle unalloyed by private gain or personal vanity, he threw himself into it wholeheartedly.

That the whole thing was another misunderstanding, like his misreading of what he'd stumbled on in Enid's desk that time, calculated to perpetuate the chain of confusions that mistake had started, was beside the point. It in no way lessened or compromised the moral worth of what he did. Whose fault was it, the misunderstanding? Ultimate blame might be laid at the door of André Breton, who coined the term "black humor." At any rate, someone unfamiliar with it had heard that a black humorist was looking at a house on traditionally lily-white Benson Road, repeated the news to one of her neighbors, and the confusion was on and the gossip flew. And a cabal of night-riding homeowners went into action.

Whenever such a threat had arisen in the past, the vigilantes had chipped in and bought up the house in question themselves, to sell it later to someone suitably white, usually at a profit. Three property owners were particularly determined that real estate values there would not be debased. They were Appetitio, an Italian paving contractor; a Pole actually named Buttinski, who owned a flourishing Cadillac-Oldsmobile agency; and the proprietor of a nursery and landscaping service named Jowett. Hearing that the consortium was secretly moving to make the purchase, Swirling leaped into action himself. He first went to do battle with Mr. Buttinski.

"I'm glad you came to discuss it openly," Buttinski told him, after pouring them each a glass of beer. "I wan tudda have a discussion with you after hearing you're the one who's been agitating against us."

"I ain't an agitator," Swirling answered, deeming it wise to avoid an egghead impression such as might set the other's back up.

Buttinski seemed to sense the parody. His beady eyes narrowed to near-invisibility as he said, "You're intelligent I'm sure, and can appreciate that when a man works all his life to carve out a place in the sun for his family he don't want it threatened. I do it for my family. Of my three daughters," he went on, waving a hand at their pictures on the grand piano, "two are at the best schools. The third, she don't wanna go to college."

"You can't win them all." Swirling took a swig of his beer, rolling an eye around at the borax furniture crowding the living room where they sat — gaudily upholstered convulsively carved sofas and chairs that probably no black negotiant would possess the equal of. Still, what did it mat-

182

ter? He must push on. Bringing his fist down on a cushion of the zebra-striped sofa he occupied, he said, "Why do you say 'threaten'? Who's threatening you, and what with? What threat does this black family pose to yours? Are you afraid their sons might rape your daughters? Or worse, marry them?"

Christ, this was going too far, even granted he had time only to paint matters in a few broad strokes. But Buttinski seemed to take no offense.

"No, no, no," he laughed. "Nuttin' so drastic. Me, I'm as democratic as they come. I believe there are good and bad in all people. I'm as democratic as they come. If it wasn't for property values, and also for the fact that mingling like this increases hostility between the races — look at the fights they're having in two integrated schools in this state right now — if it wasn't for all that, personally I wouldn't mind a bit a family of coloreds moving in right next door to me. I like to see them be a credit to their race."

Among the biodegradable dreams of early youth had been Swirling's hope that he might make it as an actor. His sense of craft told him now that, were this a scene being rehearsed, the director would have had him splutter a mouthful of his beer on hearing Buttinski's last remark. He would have been told to pick up his glass on "family of coloreds," in readiness to be seen in the act of drinking from it when Buttinski delivered his absolutely self-pillorying howler. Then he would choke on it, to depict flabbergastation. He tried sincerely to find in Buttinski some element of the human decency he was out to espouse, and not to think what other Benson Roaders must have said on first learning that Buttinski himself was buying a house here: "There goes the neighborhood."

"Blockbusters they call them," Buttinski was saying, going on to elucidate a penetration technique. "The first family buying a house in a white neighborhood is part of a deliberate plot to drive values down, see, so that other blacks can buy at prices tumbling in their favor, as the whites sell and move out."

"Why, Mr. Buttinski, that's paranoid."

"Isn't it though. Not that you can blame them, necessarily. I mean those are the simple facts, which both races are up against. It's a war, and you can talk yourself a blue streak in the face, but the prejudice is mutual. These gang fights cropping up in integrated neighborhoods and schools prove it. You can't legislate that out of the human heart." Buttinski shrugged and smiled. "So what do you want me to do?"

"I want you to cease and desist with this Fine Properties Association activity. I want you to dissolve the cabal."

Buttinski gazed off into a corner of the ceiling, holding a mouthful of beer before swallowing it.

"The what?"

"Cabal. A cabal is a conspiratorial group of plotters or intriguers, also the secret scheme or plot itself. The word derives from the French *cabale*, that in turn from the medieval Latin *cabbala*. The term was popularized during the reign of Charles II, when it was applied to the ministry of Clifford, Arlington, Buckingham, Ashley and Lauderdale, whose initials, as you perceive, form the acronym for the word."

"Sheesh."

Swirling drew a deep breath and went grimly forward. This Jasper would not be let off lightly. There was more.

"A Cabala, often spelled uppercase, is also an occult theosophy of rabbinical origin, widely transmitted in medieval Europe, based on an esoteric interpretation of the Hebrew Scriptures."

"Some of my best friends are Jews. One of my daughters dates a boy named Pincus."

"That will not be enough. I want you to dissolve your cabal, under pain of legal reprisal to be waged also against the sanctimonious real estate board with which you are in collusion, or cahoots, and terminate instantly your nefarious subterranean activities." Swirling plowed remorselessly on, deciding to abandon all mealymouthed accommodation and unmask himself as an egghead, as suspected, and also that target maligned by reactionaries, a bleeding-heart liberal. Why are conservatives never bleeding hearts, hah? Hah? Don't they have any? Any hearts maybe? Hah? Fired by this line of thought, Swirling delivered his peroration, as it were, watching Buttinski crumble and disintegrate in his chair under the rain of sesquipedalian animadversion.

"Sheesh," Buttinski breathed again when Swirling had finished knocking him and all his ilk. "I've been called names before, but not on that scale. You sure got a lip on you, fella. Sorry my missus ain't here to get a load of you. She reads books, likes to meet well-spoken people, tries to drag me to band-shell concerts at the Peavey Pavilion. Well, no hard feelings," he said, rising at length. "As Abraham Lincoln said, 'I disagree with what you say but will defend to the death your right to say it.'"

"Check."

His interview with Appetitio was hardly more productive of anything, except insofar as this crusade seemed to be bringing out all his latent ethnic prejudices. "It's a too bad we have all this trouble," he mimicked Appetitio to a bar companion, a chap who had read a newspaper account of, and now admired, the fight Swirling was waging on behalf of a black something or other nobody had as yet laid eyes on. "It's a change the whole complexion of the neighborhood." That was when Swirling had called Appetitio and his lot lumpenbourgeoisie, and Appetitio had been quite impressed with the ring of that.

Swirling had expected brickbats, indeed secretly hoped for them as an aid to dramatizing the cause, but not in as literal a sense as turned out to be the case (as though the Krazy Kat influence were quite definitely abroad). A house brick sailed through his window that night, or rather through Enid's window, as he sat in the studio living room having a nightcap and resting from the exertions of another round of pushups. He had brushed his teeth and was enjoying the Pepsodent liqueur aftertaste of the bourbon, as was his bedtime wont. After coming through the skylight, the brick landed some ten feet away, having bounced across the floor in a tinkling shower of glass. A note was attached to it by a length of twine. His fame as a champion of the underdog had spread quickly, thanks to prompt publicity in the Avalon weekly *Town Crier*, which had got behind him, and he had fully anticipated some vengeful response to his crusade. He smiled as he sat a moment longer trying to imagine what crude scurrility must be scribbled on the note, and savoring his martyrdom. "Save our neighborhood," or "Down with bleeding hearts," or "Go to Africa if you don't like it here," or something of the sort no doubt.

He set his glass down and walked over and tore the note from the brick. It read:

"We're with you fellow! 100%. The world needs people like you. You're what will deliver this to you — a brick! Carry on guy!"

That was Friday, about eleven o'clock. On Sunday, along about midnight, he was reading in bed when a rock sailed through the window there and bounced all the way across the floor, coming to rest against the wainscoting. It too had a message appended to it. Swirling climbed out of bed and picked his way among the fragments of glass to where it lay. This time the note read: "Bigotry chews out loud! It must go! Hang in there man! We're with you all the way! Keep fighting the good fight!"

As he stooped to sweep up the scraps of windowpane, using a shirt cardboard for a dustpan, he wondered who his cohorts were, and how much more show of support he could stand. Why did they skulk under his chamber window or shoot by the house like night riders in flaming demonstrations of unity?

Flaming was good. Because the metaphor, too, took literal form in the shape of a burning arrow that next flew over the rooftop and impaled a table umbrella on the back terrace where Swirling was giving lunch to the lady journalist who had been writing him up, charring one of its plastic segments as well as part of the note wired to the shaft of the arrow. All that could be made out was, "—r—cause needs a martyr, bu—-ake care of yourself! Prejudice must go!"

Bessie Grinder was editor of the *Town Crier,* and wife of the publisher. In addition to giving Swirling's fight on discrimination a good news play, running front-page stories on the stink he had single-handedly stirred up, she was writing a profile on him personally — as a pillar of the community who was also an art collector, wine connoisseur and amateur cook. For his baching days he had really had only one specialty: a takeout carton of Chinese food overturned on a grilled steak. But he had now learned to bake a quiche Lorraine. They were having it there, tête-à-tête, with a bottle of Neuchâtel. Bessie Grinder was an ash-blonde in her forties, with soft gray eyes that had been returning his own speculative gaze. He had met her before, working together on one of the charity committees whose hours of tedium he had seen as expiation for his adulteries, and one of the bonuses of which, in turn, had been the chance to meet new women. "Sterling Swirling" they were calling him (reviving the metaphor of a set of fine flatware some, if not most, of which was missing). So cause and effect, punishment and reward had ceaselessly rotated and intertwined, spiraling to focus on this fragrant spring Sunday afternoon, with all its shimmering probabilities. He had kissed her before, and was now justly confident of complete acquiescence. She had been unmistakably telegraphing as much by word, look and

187

gesture. The rumor that she was round-heeled was not one he felt he had a right to be put off by; and hearsay that Jack Grinder was insanely jealous and equivalently dangerous didn't deter him. There were so few pleasures in a life so short, and this was the best.

The latest note having been pored and puzzled over, they returned to the interview.

"Look, I'd like to have a photographer come and take some shots of you. Posing in front of your art collection —"

"They're all in storage, unfortunately. My life has been rather a shambles lately, you know —"

"Yes, I know."

"— and what with all the burglaries around, and moving from house to house without alarm systems, I felt it best to put everything in a safe place. Not just robberies, but vandalism. God knows what all."

Bessie struck the tabletop. "The Sidewinders! Of course. That's where this arrow came from, and the other crazy notes. That was a motorcycle we heard as it came over the house. They're a bunch of crypto-revolutionaries who don't *want* the bourgeoisie to patch up its own rotten system, et cetera. They want it to collapse, and a new society to start things all over again. They're Maoists, among other things."

"Aha. Then that's it. Well, the humor with which they go about it is both perverted and subtle. Some sense of irony. They're worse than the Yippies of a few years back. Remember them?"

"Yes, but look. I don't think we'd better bring that into the story. Make it complicated and fuzzy. Confuse people. We'll just say your house has been the object of attack from straight hate bigots. And anonymous phone calls. What do they say, by the way?"

"Knock it off, we want to preserve the neighborhood. Lot of obscenities. They aren't the Sidewinders. They're just straight know-nothings."

"By the way, I'd like to interview the family who are trying to buy the house. Do you know who they are, or where?"

"No. Nobody's seen them, to my knowledge. It'd seem a little mysterious except that the house itself is empty and the owners are heirs living in the Middle West somewhere. That's why it's taking so long to get the deal off the ground, and why nobody's on the scene. But the cabal is doing everything it can to screw the transaction up, you can be sure of that. How about another bottle? Shall we have it here or" — the definitive pass must be thrown — "take it to bed with us?"

Bessie Grinder closed her notebook and folded her arms on top of it with what was only mock severity.

"Look, first we've got to pin you down. The benefit fashion show for the NAACP is all set. In fact it's only a month off. I agreed to head the committee and even have it at my house. Jack's going along with that, and also tying the whole thing in with this civil rights to-do. He's putting the paper behind it. We've got enough local merchants and New York department stores to supply the clothes. Tickets are already going like hotcakes. What we don't have is an emcee."

"I —"

"Let me finish. That's what you've told I don't know how many benefits and washed out at the last minute. You copped out on Birth Defects, Cancer, Heart Association, name it."

"Well, that was because I wasn't sure I had enough material worked up, or I had worries, problems, crises. But I won't cop out on the National Association for the Advancement of Colored People. Or you."

"You solemnly swear to go the works, whole hog? Do it as Groucho Marx and everything?"

"I promise."

"O.K. Now I'll have that other bottle with you."

189

Thirteen

THE FASHION SHOW LUNCHEON was held outdoors on the five-acre Grinder estate. The weather was perfect, the models the most beautiful obtainable in Avalon, and the event a sellout. The only thing was that the *cause célèbre* around which the whole gala was built had been knocked out from under it. There was no Negro family trying to move into town at all. Only a dapper little author of comedies in which terminal cancer patients had their beds short-sheeted by fun-loving hospital inmates, women shot prowlers thinking they were their husbands, and manhole covers blew up in people's faces. And he a pale imitation of most reigning black humorists of the hour at that.

Jack Grinder was furious. He had been made a fool of both professionally and personally. As publisher of the *Town Crier* he had adopted a crusading stance by giving prime coverage to the mare's nest into which Swirling had marched them, and then supplemented that with a profile of this "champion of the underdog and local connoisseur." As a private citizen he had flamboyantly thrown open his house and grounds to the fashion benefit, an extra gesture made as a reconstructed Southerner prospering in New England. His anger was hardly tempered by the discovery that the chef of this preposterous stew was making love to his wife. And now the last straw: having to splutter his protestations to a doubled-over simulacrum of a movie clown in a tailcoat, wire glasses, greasepaint eyebrows and mustache, brandishing a fat cigar as he prowled among his, Grinder's, flower beds, ogling the women including, and especially, his wife.

"It's no egg on your face," Grinder said, zigzagging in the bounder's wake up and down the paths and stairways of his multilevel property. "Know what I think? I think you knew it all the time."

"Not true. The yolk's on me too. Ah, hello, Mrs. For- sythe, how are you? How's your husband's *Weltschmerz?* Better I hope."

"Champion of the underdog and dilettante of art! Know what I think? I think you're a dilettante of the downtrodden. And look out for those daffodils."

"Why? They don't look dangerous to me. Well, well, Har- riet Tolliver, in the flesh — and believe me that's the way I like you." He flirted his eyebrows lewdly as he took a sharp left around a pachysandra bed.

"Why, you —!" Grinder persisted.

"Why me?"

"I've half a mind —"

"If that. Ah, my petite. Headed for the punch bowl, dear? You go your way and I'll go your way."

"I'd like to know something."

"So would I if I were you. Hi, baby, think you'll have anything on tonight?"

"I hope for your sake you're drunk," Grinder called out, letting him go for the moment.

Everyone within earshot smiled, thinking this was all part of the act. Grinder was going over big as a stooge for Groucho. "You ought to be in pictures, Jack," someone laughed. That was how Swirling thought it best to play it himself, though he knew Grinder wasn't fooling but meant business. Swirling had in fact bolstered himself with a few drinks, in addition to popping back a Dexamyl, and was beginning early on to feel a little giddy. He must try to hold this plateau, neither going too high nor skidding into a letdown before he had to take the mike.

Grinder watched him climb a brick stairway to the main terrace, where he slithered in and out of a line of women queued up for the champagne punch bowl, at which Bessie Grinder was officiating, in an ice-blue gown that would certainly be called stunning by the commentator. He kept up a steady rain of suggestively flirtatious comments and asides, accompanied by smirks and twitches of his eyebrows and flicks of his cigar. He rolled his eyes till you could see their whites a mile off. Bessie laughingly poured him a cup of punch. "Say when," she said.

"What's the matter with right now?" he said, jiggling his eyebrows salaciously. "You'll find me in the parlor waiting. Or if you expect to be tied up for a while, how about Mrs. Diamond here? Would you care to join me, Mrs. Diamond?"

"Will you be good?"

"I'll be sensational."

Mrs. Diamond, a stout woman in a purple pants suit, giggled, delighted to be the object of all this ribaldry. "You seem a red-blooded all-American handful all right."

"Yes. I take a cold shower every morning and feel rosy all day. Rosy's out of town just now and so I thought I'd try to scare up something here. So lead on. You go your way and I'll go your way."

But Jack Grinder was coming his way now, and he lit out. Grinder was angrier than ever, growing in the part, so that people said, "You're a better foil for him than Margaret Dumont."

There was no lack of Margaret Dumont types on hand, on whom Groucho pounced whenever they hove into view. "Ada Morgenstern! I don't see nearly enough of you, even in that décolletage. What do you say to a moonlight skinny dip some night? Tonight? Splendid. Nine-ish, then, at the beach. Later we can go to my place and I'll show you my record albums. We'll play a few overtures and then I'll make some . . ."

Sailing as close to the wind as that required picking his dowagers with a little more tact than, in fact, he did. He had been back to the punch bowl twice more by the time the fashion show started, and that added to the state of flushed excitement with which he took the mike to start the proceedings. The mike was hooked up at the head of a flight of stairs leading down to the pool around which the models were to strut. He first made a few remarks about the importance of the cause they were all there to support. Concluding with, "And if there's one thing I'd like to drive home today, it's that blonde in the red dress at Table Seven." Then he introduced the commentator for the show, a local disc jockey he called "a man about town and perennial weekender. Hostesses all find him totally absorbing. He's such a sponge." Turning to the subject himself, a natty young man in white slacks and blue blazer, he said, "They tell me you have charisma. You certainly don't look well. Are you taking anything for it?"

Having turned over the mike, he by no means retired from the scene. He kibitzed both the commentator and the models parading around the pool. He twitted the affected color designations. A line of dresses came in "bone, toast and pomegranate." "What ever happened to white, brown and red?" he razzed, provoking a sympathetic titter from the audience, seated over their coffee at the luncheon tables. A "front slit suit skirt" billed as "ideal for tramping on the moors" was an open invitation to disaster. "Ah, my dear," he said, prowling along beside the model as she minced her way around the pool, "come away with me, over that stone wall and across that beautiful cattle pasture. Slipshod through the cowslip in your front slit suit skirt. All together, everybody! Slipshod through the cowslip in your front slit suit skirt." Then a line of maternity clothes for which suitably pregnant local women had been recruited elicited such gratuities as, "Your slip is showing. Who's the father? Or are you telling?" He skulked in the wake of a young woman modeling "expectation slacks." "That's a perfect fit. Which is what your husband will have when he finds out about us." He took a puff on the cigar and sang. "Yes, sir, that's my baby. . ."

Very little if any of this set well with the merchants who had lent the garments for the occasion, since it distracted attention from the wares to their contents. One donor, the proprietor of a boutique called Glad Rags, a man named Carl Framer, finally stepped up and protested openly, whereupon Swirling switched from lubricious innuendo back again to straight insolence. "You'd make a perfect stranger," he said. Then to the audience, twitching a thumb at him, "He has lots of polish. And he should be out shining shoes with it. Well, no matter. It's as broad as it's long. And so, if I may say so, is he."

At this point he began to raise eyebrows other than his own. A man visibly determined to take a firmer line than the owner of Glad Rags stepped over.

"I'm Gaylord Haines."

"I've got troubles of my own."

"From the Lord and Taylor branch?"

"Maybe you can help me. I'm looking for something in a bathing suit. Oh, there she is. Thanks just the same. Come, my dear, we must fly. The railroads are all bankrupt. I tell you I'm at the end of my tether. Because my wife's at the other end. Our son threw up in a restaurant the other day, and she said, 'That's enough out of you.'"

The man from Lord and Taylor now began stalking in Groucho's wake, as Groucho tailed still another dish, thus making for a rather ludicrous procession. At the same time, the commentator got his note cards mixed up and was extolling some cocktail separates though a pair of culottes was being modeled. Things fell apart, the center could not hold.

"Just a minute," the man from Lord and Taylor said. "This is a worthy cause of course, and we all cooperate. But you understand we do like something we can count on."

"Of course. I'll send you an abacus in the morning. But don't bother me now. I'm trying to get the lay of the land — if I can find out who she is. They tell me you're a boulevardier. I'm a Baptist myself, but I always say what difference does it make what denomination we belong to since we all worship the same god — money."

They couldn't get him to sit down — except in somebody's lap. And here Grinder, recognizing allies for his own disapproval, resumed a show of truculence that was emphatically refueled when Bessie was called on to parade her ice-blue gown. Swirling, with the best of intentions, and in what he honestly thought was good fun, took the occasion to interject a word of thanks to their gracious hosts — an ideally married couple. "They're happy, and why shouldn't they be? They have a lot in common. And a lot more in preferred." Grinder took this to be a gibe at what everyone there knew, his having married into money, and his now living as lord of the manor on another family's wealth. "She comes from good stock, the best. A. T. and T., DuPont, General Motors. Name it. Bessie and I met on a plane coming back from Paris. We were an hour in a holding pattern over Kennedy. I hated to let her go."

Swirling was oblivious to any offense in his words, being

swept along on a tide of emotions completely his own, and in which he was in a sense eerily detached from the very scene he was creating.

He had reached a crest of exhilaration that could only be described as an overpowering sensation that he *was* Groucho Marx. He had become what he was impersonating. The conviction was irresistible that he was vacating the shell of himself for that of another. He put his arm around Bessie Grinder saying, "I gather your husband is an art collector. He asked me a while ago what I thought of Dubuffet, and I said, 'I haven't eaten anything off of it yet, but lead me to it, I'm starved.' I'm also starved for affection. Are you starved for affection? We could make beautiful music together. Do you like breakfast in bed too? She likes breakfast in bed. Give her orange juice, coffee, and a roll in the hay anytime."

Grinder was a burly enough man, but rage seemed to have swollen him up to twice his normal size. He looked like one of the glowering heavies of the early motion pictures, as he shook his fist at Swirling and came at him in a mood now not to be trifled with or misunderstood. Swirling took to his heels and headed for the house, as the quickest way of getting the scene now definitely in the making at least out of view of the guests. They had stopped laughing, a bit put out, and not exactly sure what to make of it all. Had it been planned this way from the first? Was this part of the act, this climax that seemed so horribly real?

Swirling shot through the front door, looked around in all directions, made off along a corridor to the left. He popped into a closet just as Grinder rounded the turn after him. When Grinder opened the door, Swirling said, "Hi. I'm a closet heterosexual," and ducking under Grinder's uplifted arm, scuttled along the corridor smack into a part of the house the models were using as a dressing room. Girls and young women in varying stages of dishabille squealed in surprise.

"Well, I never," one said, holding a dress up to her front. "Oh, come now, you don't expect us to believe that, do you?" Swirling said, circling around behind her to keep a table between himself and the now genuinely boiling Grinder.

After one orbit of the table, he had his next move planned. At Grinder's back were a pair of French doors leading to another, smaller terrace, and just beyond that could be glimpsed a bathhouse for use in connection with the pool. It had once possibly served as a toolshed or something. Maneuvering about till their positions in relation to the table were reversed, and the doors were behind him, Swirling wheeled around and shot through them, across the terrace, and straight for the bathhouse, firing a last *double entendre* over his shoulder.

Three concrete stairs led to the half-open door of the bathhouse. He tried to take all three at one long, balletic leap from the patch of grass that intervened, to maintain the wooziness of farce the scene had been so far satisfactorily accumulating, but he missed. The toe of his shoe slipped off the edge of the top stair tread, causing him to lose his balance and sprawl face-forward with a force that both twisted his ankle and cut a deep gash across its shinbone on the rim of the middle stair. So the approach of Grinder found him sitting on the grass, nursing his leg.

"Get up like a man," Grinder panted, "so I can knock you down again."

Swirling hiked up a torn trouser-leg and inspected his injuries. His ankle was bleeding profusely from a wound already swollen and discolored. He looked up at Grinder, a grimace of pain distorting the grin with which he inquired, with an insolence still wholly in character, "I trust you're insured, my good man?"

"I'll sue *you*," Grinder snorted. "You'd better believe it, you two-timing — For slander. For defamation of character.

You meant those things, goddam you. I demand satisfaction. My wife demands satisfaction."

"Every night? You lucky dog."

Grinder placed a hand to his brow and executed a half pirouette to communicate the general concept of disbelief. Swirling was experiencing sensations other than those related to his mishap. With a vestigial flicker of identity as himself, like the final fading spark of a dying fire, he felt that he had now transcended mere impersonation and soared into true parody, that art that calls for the tricky creation, within the audience, of the illusion that the subject has on his own Gone Too Far. Thus if Groucho's stock-in-trade was insult and outrage, then he must himself appear to have graduated this trait into the unforgivable. Judging from the eggplant color dangerously suffusing Grinder's face, as though apoplectic seizure might be in the offing, Swirling would seem to have achieved that end.

Several others had been attracted by the to-do, and were about equally divided between looking after Swirling and trying to mollify Grinder. Bessie and a model in a beach coat helped Swirling to his feet, or foot rather, as no weight could be put on the other, and then assisted him in hopping on one leg to a chair on the terrace. It occurred to nobody to bring the chair to him. Grinder was still rumbling, though less menacingly. "— the shape he's in now. But I intend to sue you for every nickel you've got."

"Oh, that won't be necessary, old bean," Swirling said, pausing on one leg. "I'll gladly give them to you." Digging what loose change he had from his pocket, he fished out three nickels and tossed them nonchalantly into the air. "Here you are, old chap, that's the lot."

Now that he stood up, the blood was seen to be pouring down his shoe, and so not only was he hurried into the chair, but another was dragged over for him to put his foot up on, propped on a couple of cushions to raise it as high as possible. That soon reduced the bleeding to a mere trickle.

"We've got to get him to a doctor," Bessie said.

"No, to a hospital," Grinder said, still panting. "He'll have to have it sewed up."

"Everybody in stitches, eh?" Swirling grinned, and the blonde in the beach coat wrung her hands with a low moan of appreciation and said, "Absy incredible." Bessie ran into the house to call for the town ambulance as somebody else came out with a wet towel to pack around the injury. The pain caused by all these ministrations, as well as that experienced when he had first heaved himself erect, left the possibility that the leg might be more than sprained. "Now we're all fractured," Swirling said, spiritually rummaging in the blonde's beach coat as she again wrung her hands and murmured, "Absy fantastic." Someone in the swelling crowd Grinder was trying in vain to shoo back to the festivities whispered, "I think he's delirious." "Or drunk," someone else said. "Or both," added a third. "Come on, come on, let's all go back, shall wě?" Grinder called out.

As they waited for the ambulance, Swirling sensed there was something wrong. Something was missing. What was it? Of course. His eye wandered along the lawn toward the bathhouse and spotted what he was looking for. "Would somebody get me my cigar? It's right over there."

The blonde in the beach coat went to retrieve it, instantly throwing it away. "You can't smoke that. Have you got a fresh cigar, Jack?" Rolling his eyes to heaven, again to convey incredulity, Grinder went into the house, returning presently with a humidor, which he extended, open, to Swirling.

"Thanks, old boy."

Swirling was chewing on the cigar when the ambulance came wailing up the driveway, followed by a police car with an officer who had been radioed to help the driver get the patient onto a stretcher and into the ambulance. A young woman attendant rode with Swirling, a registered nurse who was the daughter of the driver, who owned the ambulance.

"You can't take that cigar in with you," she said. "There's an oxygen tank in there."

She relented on learning it would not be lit. On the way to the hospital she asked him a few routine questions, his age, blood type in case he needed a transfusion, which she doubted. "What's your type?"

"You're my type."

"Your blood type."

"I'm not positive. So I must be negative. How about a little music to lighten things up, macushla? Do you know the Hemoglobin Song? Hemoglobin, oh my darling, when the lights are dim and low. . ."

"All right, Groucho, what's the matter?"

She was disturbed at the way he had broken off, clutching at his chest. She bent her head to listen, at the same time taking his pulse.

"You're fibrillating," she said. "Too much strain and excitement? What the devil's been going on back there? Must be some party!"

"Fibrillating. I've heard that term. What is it?"

"Rapid pulsations, usually of the auricles, which the ventricles schlep along with as best they can. Nothing to it, but very scary at the time. When it stops —"

"Stops she says. You're a cheerful little earful."

"No, I mean when the incident's over you'll throw up this perfect cardiogram. But be quiet. Let me get your pulse." She looked at her wristwatch. Could she count fast enough to measure the flutter against her fingertips? In his breast was no longer a smoothly throbbing engine but a clump of writhing worms. She set his hand back on the blanket with a shrug. She had seen worse cases than this snap out of fib in no time.

"Have you ever fibrillated before?"

"No, but then I've never had a nurse like you before. What's the gallop?"

"A hundred seventy-five. Maybe two hundred. I had a niece used to go into fib, and her pulse was sometimes over two hundred. I once had a four hundred. Like a hummingbird's wing. Don't worry about it. They'll convert you at the hospital before you know it."

"Is it that bad?"

She laughed. "No, no, not that kind of conversion. Like running in with a priest or anything. It's the term they use for getting a patient back to normal. Medical jargon. Few doses of Inderal or quinidine and it'll soon be back to good old seventy-two." However, she seemed to be eyeing the oxygen tank. She rose and reached for the cone. "Why, do you believe in God?" she asked as she set it on his nose.

"I've —" He pushed the cone away so he could answer her question. "I've heard a lot about Him, of course, and . . ." He faltered, the hand with the cigar in it falling over the edge of the stretcher.

"Yes?" She again bent to put her ear to his chest. "What?"

"And I'm . . ." The cigar dropped from his fingers. His voice sank to a whisper. This time she put her ear to his lips to catch his last words.

"You're what?"

"I'm dying to meet Him."

The Resolution

Fourteen

"SO HE DIED with a joke on his lips," Dr. Josko said.

He had learned everything he could through hypnosis, he was now reasonably sure, and had interviewed as many people concerned in the story as he could, or thought it feasible or discreet to — except for the one young woman to whom he was now putting the case in his office. Pauline Winchester. Dr. Josko thought black was beautiful about as often as white was, which wasn't very often, but here there was no room for argument. Hints that she might be pivotal in the patient's trauma had led him to seek out Mrs. Becky Swirling's cooperation in getting in touch with her. Mrs. Swirling had found Pauline's name and number in an address book in Swirling's desk, phoned, and asked her to come out. The appointment was arranged and here she was — the last lead Dr. Josko felt he had.

"Died as he lived, you might say," he went on. "Died as

Robert Swirling — as I'm convinced he thought he was doing, according to the ambulance attendant's testimony. She thought so herself. To surface as Groucho Marx. But what a bridge to delusion! What an adroit escape mechanism! Just to continue the impersonation. To stay inside it." He shook his head in admiration. "What a snug haven to curl up in, safe from the winds that buffet this cold world."

"Just what do you think I could do?' Pauline asked, crossing her shapely legs as she undid the top button of a light tunic-length red cotton coat, worn, in the cool June weather, over a pink-and-white flowered V-neck dress.

"I'm coming to that. I said he surfaced as Groucho, but it would be more accurate to say he went underground as that. What we want to do is make him surface again as Robert Swirling. Something deep inside him surely doesn't want to be left in that oubliette. Doomed to gag after gag forever." The doctor laughed. "Of course as T. S. Eliot said, there's sometimes more wisdom in music-hall jokes than in what passes for philosophy. And, I suppose, psychology."

"Eliot happened to be a fan of Groucho's."

"Oh, really? That's interesting."

"I'll just give you that piece of erudition. But getting back to Bob Swirling. He was a nice guy — and a bastard. Like most whites in their relations with blacks. It's all a crock, the whole thing's a crock," she said, and the doctor thought it best to give the militant her head. "All this jive. At least the blacks know they're jiving, but white liberals think they're being straight. They're jiving *themselves*. Give me honest backlash bigots anytime. At least they're honest. All this jive. But don't get me wrong. I like Bob Swirling. A lot. I did right off, from the start."

"Excuse me. I don't mean to interrupt, but just what is jive? I see and hear the term constantly, but I'm not sure I know what it means."

"You know what it means from the context I just used it in. It means ..." The girl shrugged. She found it as hard to define as the doctor did to grasp it. "It means playing the game. Deceptive, uh, glib or deceptive talk or attitude. Using your secret smarts to play along with somebody — the enemy, Whitey — and in so doing put one over on him. All that."

"I think I see, yes." He thought it best not to ask what a crock was, having displayed enough ignorance of the prevalent jargon for one afternoon. He dimly sensed it to mean something totally deplorable or without merit. Jesus! Psychiatric jargon was hard enough.

"Just how do you expect to make him surface again, and just where do I fit in? Of course I'll do all I can. I'd be only too glad to help, if I could see how." She unbuttoned the rest of her coat and shook it out, revealing a figure as ravishing as her face. Oh, this incessant erotic bombardment, the doctor thought. It was a crock. So was this case, probably, with the three-thousand-dollar bill already run up. But he would give it what they used to call the college try. Today it would be going for broke. Or was that outmoded too?

"My plan is as follows."

The doctor rose and began navigating his office.

"What I've found inside the patient is a psychic jungle, the most incredible tangle of guilt, remorse, anxiety, frustration, failure both professional and marital. Name it. On top of everything else was the embarrassment — and let's never underestimate plain old male human embarrassment — of the, this last incident. The crock he pulled over the civil rights tempest — a black humorist trying to move in was all! — a controversy in which, posing as a ... No, I take that back. He wasn't posing, that's unfair. He was sincere about it. Nevertheless he was the white knight on a charger who suddenly came a cropper. Now a hero, and in a twinkling a damn fool. Then with this gala benefit, going too far, and more too far, and then still more too far. Till the host, who knows he's been fooling around with his wife — Do you mind, my dear?"

Pauline collapsed with laughter in her chair. "Let's get out of Sunday school."

"Knowing what's up, threatens to sue him. Did you know that alienation of affections was still actionable here in Connecticut until very recently? Maybe Grinder thinks the law is still on the books. Or maybe it's slander he's been threatening to sue for, and maybe Swirling realized all you have to do to freeze anybody's assets harder than the polar cap here is to bring suit. I don't think you even need a judgment, though I'm not too sure about all that. In any case, Mrs. Swirling has got to Mrs. Grinder, who got to Mr. Grinder and threatened to leave him — namely, make a real public cuckold out of him — if he didn't drop the plan to sue. So that's probably resolved. The only thing is, we still have to coax Swirling out of hiding and back to reality. It's cold out here, and he knows it, but that's our job."

"How? Your plan, *s'il vous plait*?"

"Because of all these things, Robert Swirling has been traumatized into Groucho Marx. The solution? Reverse it."

"You expect me to say 'You mean —?' I'll say it. So, you mean?"

"Yes. Traumatize Groucho Marx back into Robert Swirling."

"You mean scare the bejesus out of him in some way so that he'll, like, scuttle back into Swirling? How?"

"That's where you come in."

"But you've still got me on hold, man. How?"

With the most excruciatingly cheerful grin the doctor shrugged, heaving his shoulders up and spreading his arms abroad.

"I don't know. I thought you might have some ideas."

She sat for some time in concentrated thought, leaning forward with an elbow propped on a knee and her chin in her hand. She clearly relished the challenge, as much for polemic as therapeutic reasons, one could bank on that. The doctor watched her with wary anticipation, now both excited and dubious about this unorthodox venture in shock treatment; fearing as much as hoping the imp would come up with something. From the patient's mesmerized account he remembered her tendentious shenanigans with Mrs. Pesky at the door, the acid little charade with the broom. Swirling had characterized her well: delicious; beguiling; wicked; sly. Whatever she cooked up would have to satisfy the need to score off Whitey simultaneously with bringing him round. Why did she have anything to do with him — Whitey as such, that is? To draw him in closer for the special change she rang on the sex war. Make him a more intimate candidate for her satire, and thus more vulnerable. The bed was a battleground. Twice the battleground it was for the sexes normally. What an era for that emotion once known as the Light of the World!

"I suppose it would have to be something of a sexual nature," the doctor said, then suddenly waved the entire project off with both hands, at the same time shaking his head. "No, it's off. This is too risky. We're playing with fire."

"You haven't even heard my idea yet," she said. Dismantling her Thinker pose, she sat back again, grinning. "I like practical jokes."

"I'm sure."

"What I'll do is, what I could do would be go back to bed with him. As Groucho Marx I mean. Assuming he doesn't recognize me."

"He won't. I'd stake my professional reputation on that guess," the doctor said, still swimming through the room freestyle. "But no, this is too dicey. It's tampering with. . ." He didn't know what it might be tampering with, unless it was a malpractice suit. He could see her in court testifying with relish, the same relish clearly exhibited for whatever jape she had in mind. And he hadn't even heard it yet! Now she outlined it.

"Go to bed with him, say, in a motel. Right? Just over the New York state line. Right? Though I'm twenty-two I can pass for a minor." He listened from behind her. "There'll be a knock on the door and my big brother, six and a half feet tall and weighing two hundred and twenty pounds, will be standing there, no he'll burst in, come to knock his block off unless he does right by me."

"You have such a brother?"

"No, but it'll be easy enough to find a bruiser who can act the part. I know two or three man mountains. There'll be something about turning him over to the police for violating the Mann Act, transporting a seventeen-year-old across —"

"No, no," the doctor said, still swimming against the current. "I wash my hands of it. Forget I ever —"

But she was warming to her theme, unstoppable, growing more enthusiastic with every convolution of the plot. Of which the climax was: "No, wait. I'll wait for that. Not the first time, but the second or third. Then I'll sock it to him."

The doctor stopped and regarded her apprehensively over his shoulder, in prison himself already, merely pausing in the circumnavigation of his cell. "Sock it to him?"

"Yes. The clincher. I'll whisper there's a little stranger on the way — ours. I'm pregnant. We'll be married. He'll have to marry me. Or else." She turned to the doctor with a jubilant laugh. "Then watch him head for the tall timber. Talk about taking a powder! It'll be the last of Groucho Marx. The end of the fugue. *Fini*. Back to the safe harbor of Robert Swirling. No more amnesia."

"Hmmm . . . No. No, I wash my hands of it. It's absolutely out. Out!"

"I suppose lots of girls want to sleep with you because you're Groucho Marx."

"*C'est la vie*," he said, rolling his eyes with a mooncalf expression.

They were sitting in a restaurant in the Blue Boar Motel, just off the Connecticut Turnpike. It was "their" place, this being their third stay here. For purposes of assignation, she insisted that he wear normal clothing, dispense with the facial props, and enter public establishments walking erect and without the stalking crouch, so that he wouldn't be recognized and besieged by autograph hunters and one thing and another. But voice and manner remained the same, as well as the omnivorous flirtation with women everywhere, including waitresses, to say nothing of the need to spread chaos with incessant horseplay.

"I'll have the corned beef hash," he told the waitress as he consulted the menu. "No, give me the beef tongue and spinach instead. On second thought — or is it third? — I'll take the liver and onions. I should be able to count better. I'm a certified public accountant, so I'm interested in figures, and believe me yours adds up."

"You should *be* certified," the waitress said.

"Well, that cleans me out. I'm all washed up."

When the liver and onions came he said it was wrong.

"But that's what you ordered," the waitress said.

"Instead of the beef tongue and spinach. This is instead of the corned beef hash. Speaking of numbers again, are you in the book? Can I have yours? You know you've got mine."

Everything else was rigidly in order for the climactic scene. Pauline's "brother" waited outside in a car, a strapping friend six and a half feet tall who shared her taste for pranks, especially those with social content. The hoax was assembled in every detail, ready to roll. He was to surprise the lovers at exactly nine o'clock, and for that hour she timed her revelation about the bundle from heaven apparently en route.

"Are you sure?" Groucho said, drawing back in consternation from the murmured confidence.

"Positive," she whispered. Her voice was gentle as the rustle of the sheets, though that rose to a considerable commotion as he backed out of bed, blanching. "The doctor says there's no doubt. Oh, aren't you secretly — glad, Groucho?"

"Jesus, *glad?* You must be — I must be —"

"Dreaming?" she said helpfully, sitting up. "That the whole thing is a dream from which you'll awaken and find everything O.K.?"

"I thought you were taking care of it."

"I guess I . . . secretly wanted your child. Groucho Marx's child. You'll acknowledge it, won't you? To the whole world? I mean you wouldn't be such a —"

Just then there was a loud banging on the door, and a voice in the corridor boomed, "Pauline? Open up! This is Jumbo. I know you're in there. And that rat with you."

"Oh, my God," she said, springing out of bed herself. "It's my brother, Jumbo. He — he knows about it. He's been suspecting us, and, well, I had to tell him. He made me. He'd have killed me — and he'll kill you too if he thinks you'd try to weasel out of it."

Groucho shot a look at the closet — vain reflex!

"Jumbo's old-fashioned. Sex to him is sacred. This is no mere bagatelle."

"I bagatelle out of here," Groucho said through chattering teeth as he climbed into his trousers. His shirt was already on, and he stuffed the tails wildly into his pants, his eye on the window. It overlooked a projecting rooftop, he didn't

212

know how far down. They were on the topmost of three floors.

Pauline pretended to be spinning around in a panic herself, though she did start for the door.

"Don't open it for God's sake!"

"It won't stop him. He'll just walk through it, like King Kong. Matchwood. That temper of his. Once in a bar fight he hit a man over the head with a bottle of muscatel."

"I muscatel out of here."

"He's a Black Panther, have I told you? This between us isn't just a man and a woman, it's exploitation. On your part of course. To Jumbo the ultimate showdown will be the showdown between blacks and whites. That'll be it. Armageddon."

"Armageddon the hell out of here."

Using two fingers for a shoehorn Groucho got into his oxfords. Stuffing his socks into his pockets he heard the rumbling beyond the door rise to a steadily more ominous pitch.

"I know you're in there and who you are! I'll get you, Groucho Marx. On a bastardy charge, you bastard! I'll make your name mud. But first I'll get you arrested on a Mann Act charge, transporting a minor across the state line. I'll get you on statutory rape. But first I'll hand you your head. I'll peel your face off and stuff it down your throat. I'll break a couple of your arms and then your neck, and when I'm through with that —"

He slid the window up and looked down. It was perhaps twenty feet to the pebble-tar rooftop below. It would be a risk. He might break a leg. But that would be nothing to what he'd sustain if he stayed here, according to the catalogue of mayhems Jumbo was still enumerating in the passage, to the accompaniment of kettledrum thumps on the door. He kneed over the sill, looked down, and jumped.

He rolled to his right after hitting the roof, which some-what broke his fall, so that he landed over on one haunch without spraining or breaking anything. He scrambled to his feet and made for the edge of the roof, where, peering down, he saw what he already knew — that he was only halfway to the ground. He spotted a drainpipe at one corner and slid hastily down that. He plunged through some shrubbery and lit out across a short stretch of lawn toward the motel parking lot. It was while sprinting across its asphalt surface as fast as his legs could carry him that Swirling became quite himself again, though without knowing where he was, how he had got there, what he was doing there, or why he seemed to be streaking up a driveway toward a roadside sign blinking out the words "Blue Boar — Vacancy" in red neon letters.

Fifteen

"NOW HERE'S A CHANCE to really strike a blow for integration, Biff."

It was some weeks later, and Pauline and Swirling were lunching cozily once again at the Museum of Modern Art, where they had first met. Things were fairly back to normal. The two-month blank in Swirling's mind had been gradually filled in. Enid and Leo had returned from Provence and were back in the house on Benson Road, the neighborhood now enhanced by a pink-cheeked black humorist of Welsh-Irish extraction who was widely praised by critics for his laugh-only-when-it-hurts *Weltanschauung*. He hadn't known he had such a thing until he came across it in print. Swirling's father and stepmother were selling her house and moving into a Florida condominium, fixed for life on what the property and the Power Skower between them had netted. The old couple were very compatible, in nothing more so than their common and often expressed wish to "get back to the status quo." What had ever happened to it? To the time when families lived happily together, when the dollar was worth a hundred cents, when there were two sexes and Republican Presidents kept the national debt down to within reason and rugged individualism in a free country gave everyone a chance to be something besides a number on a punch card. That was the status quo, and it was gone now — gone with the wind. It would never come back. Becky was flourishing in her brokerage business (the sale of Mrs. Pesky's two buildings had made for a fat commission). The affair with Bessie Grinder was not taken up again, and with that assurance Jack Grinder called off his dogs. There would be no suit. The only fly in the ointment was Pauline's gossip now.

"The fact is, I *am* pregnant," she said.

Comic-strip artists depict speechless consternation by enclosing the legend GULP in the dialogue balloon over the character's head, and actors also when called upon to embody dire discombobulation swallow hard, sometimes audibly. But Swirling's throat was so dry he couldn't swallow, being too floored to manage anything but the same pallor with which he had greeted the news in its false form in the motel room, as his own Doppelgänger. This was the last as-if-in-a-dream occurrence of the entire course of events through which he had been drawn. Specifically, it was as if someone had pulled a plug from his throat in time for him to gurgle, "But."

"But what? Childbirth is the most natural thing in the world, silly." Was she going to get hysterical again and show him her uvula?

Swirling then did gulp, at the same time parting his hands and fluttering his fingers, as though he were running off a scherzo on an invisible piano.

"But it wouldn't . . . I mean it's an interesting moral question. Casuistry. Like something the Catholic Church would like to get its teeth into. Especially Jesuits. They love that sort of thing, Jesuits. They call it casuistry, those fine border-line moral points." Actually the Canadian border came to his mind as she said:

"Go on, honey. What are you trying to say? About casuistry and fine moral technicalities and all?"

"Wouldn't it be —?" He abandoned the craven subjunctive. "Isn't it Groucho's child?"

"But that ghost has been laid. Oh, I like that! Did you hear what I just . . . ?"

She put her head back and sent a flow of laughter gently toward the ceiling, so that he could see across the table and behind the dazzling row of teeth into the moist pink orifice of her mouth and, yes, there it was, her uvula. Quivering like a tuning fork. Then she became sober again. She leaned forward and tapped his nose with a clean spoon. "Now's the chance to show your colors. Not your color, your colors." There was no show of malice now; she seemed purged of hostility. Or at least it was repressed. There was nothing political in her adding: "It should be around the first of March."

"Of course I'll marry you, Pauline, if that's what you want."

What she wanted really was to hear him say that. She herself wasn't too keen on marriage, that now rather ramshackle institution. She wasn't even sure she wanted to marry at all. She counted among her own circle of acquaintances one or two "elective miss mothers," as the rapidly proliferating social anthropologists called women who voluntarily, and sometimes militantly, opted for having babies without taking husbands. She wanted to live with Swirling, she wanted security. Of course he would supply all of that he could financially. And that happened to be, just at that juncture, considerable. He sold the Jawlensky for sixty thousand dollars to the dealer Kobrand, who took the standard 30 percent commission as the gallery intermediary buying it for himself, the client. That left forty-two thousand dollars, which Swirling put into three savings accounts, all in his and Pauline's names jointly. Pauline would never have to worry. Now the Lord would give him quittance in full, surely?

Not quite yet.

They moved into a rented eight-room house which Becky found for them in Avalon. Now finally divorced from Swirling, she remained friendly with him, and became fast friends with Pauline, too. Pauline invited Becky to stay with them till she found a decent place of her own. It was the first sign of what proved to be Pauline's enormous gregariousness. She liked company, lots of it, all the time. Living alone with Swirling would have cramped her spirit. The two women went for walks together, rides, they shopped together, and once Swirling came home and found them romping together in the bedroom. Innocently, unabashedly. They made no bones about it, and there was no question of drawing back on being seen, much less scurrying into a closet. Then one day Becky got a long-distance phone call, and it was "Pomfret here," and *he* joined the group, bringing with him a buddy named Buddy — all making for the sort of commune Pauline loved. He was a theatrical agent Pomfret had met on the Coast and instantly cottoned to, and to whom he promptly switched professionally. There was nothing suspect in the relationship; they were just kindred spirits, and they spoke the same language — which was all Swirling needed. Buddy too was fond of the cinema rather than crazy about movies, and so on. And he showed signs of having Pomfret's staying power.

"Henry Kissinger looks like Spencer Tracy, but Spencer Tracy doesn't look in the least like Henry Kissinger," he observed one Sunday afternoon.

"Would you like to chop some wood, Buddy?" Swirling asked.

"No. I'm opposed to violence in any form."

He was a wonderful dancer, and Pauline couldn't get enough of him as a partner. An admitted change from Swirling's two left feet. So life together, there on Woodbury Street, was one long jollification. And one night, of course, there was again the Eleven O'Clock Wrap-up.

"Flash. Felonius Assault, the jazz pianist, was arrested on a morals charge in Scarsdale, New York. He was reported by two maiden ladies who testified that he had been observed eating a navel orange suggestively in front of the A and P. Flash. Robert Swirling, of this city, was awarded the Nobel Prize in medicine. Author of *The Heartbreak of Hangnail*, and leading authority on housemaid's knee, juryman's elbow and cigarette-lighter thumb. . ."

Swirling had gone upstairs a short time before, seemingly not quite himself. Now as he came down again, it was in a manner that troubled first Pauline, then Becky. "Not himself" was putting it mildly. Dressed in a double-breasted frock coat and matching dove-gray stovepipe hat, checked trousers and spats, he was drawing on a pair of lemon-yellow kid gloves. Even Mrs. Gluckstern, glancing up from the vestibule floor where she lay sprawled, sensed something amiss.

"Where are you going?" Pauline asked.

When he answered, he talked out of the side of his mouth, in an undulating nasal drawl.

"Why, my little chickadee, I fare forth for a nocturnal libation or two at the, uh, Pussy Cat Café. Don't wait up for me, my pet, 'twill be of no avail. On with the dance, let joy be unrefined. I mean unconfined."

Pomfret broke off his little caper and came over, and all exchanged apprehensive glances. Becky laughed strainedly.

"That's great," she said. "Him to a T. That gravel voice, the cadence, everything. I didn't know you were working on him."

He dug a cane out of the closet, and, bumping his head on the door, fought momentarily with his hat. Setting it to rights again, he said, "I shall make my egress now, with your leave," adding in an undertone, "if someone will remove this obnoxious quadruped from my path." The cadenced drawl, with its lingering downward inflection at the end of a phrase or a sentence, could hardly have been improved on, and even his nose seemed to grow redder, and more bulbous.

"But you can't do this!" Pauline said. She fairly shouted, as though she must by sheer volume try to penetrate the envelope of abstraction thickening rapidly about him, like an invisible cocoon; a mental sheath within which he would in a few minutes be encapsulated and inaccessible. "Come back here! You can't just run away from your responsibilities!"

He turned in the doorway and, holding the stick at chest height, with some play of the gloved fingers, smiled amiably at her.

"Why, my little chickadee, who's running? I am proceeding at a veritable stroll, as you may note for yourself. But depart I shall for the nonce, my dears . . . There's a Nubian in the fuel supply," he added in a mutter as he directed a last glance at Pomfret. "But on with the evening's gaiety, and to each his own. Let there be Jest and youthful Jollity, Quips and Cranks and wanton Wiles, Nods and Becks and wreathèd Smiles."

It was a patently happy man who, giving the crown of his hat a last jaunty tap with his fingers, sauntered down the stairs and then along the walk to the street. The night was balmy, his wallet plump, and the, uh, Pussy Cat Café lay somewhere nearby . . .

They all stood in the lighted doorway watching him go. He presently vanished from sight, flicking a scrap of litter off the sidewalk with the head of his cane as he rounded a corner.

When they were back inside the house, Pauline went straight to the telephone, looked up a number and dialed it. Becky stood by, watching, with folded arms.

"Hello. Dr. Josko? I hate to bother you at home, but. . . ."